Falling Off Cloud Nine
and
Other High Places

Lorraine Peterson

Books in this series by Lorraine Peterson

Devotionals for Teens #2

Falling Off Cloud Nine

and

Other High Places

Lorraine Peterson

BETHANY HOUSE PUBLISHERS
Minneapolis, Minnesota 55438
A Division of Bethany Fellowship, Inc.

Illustrations by LeRoy Dugan, adapted from the sketches by Neil Ahlquist

Scripture quotations are taken from the Revised Standard Version of the Bible unless otherwise noted. Used by permission.

Published by Bethany House Publishers
A Division of Bethany Fellowship, Inc.
6820 Auto Club Road, Minneapolis, Minnesota 55438

Printed in the United States of America

Library of Congress Cataloging in Publication Data

Peterson, Lorraine.
    Falling off cloud nine and other high places.

    (Devotionals for teens; #2)
    Summary: Addresses teen-age concerns and presents spiritual truths in a way which intends to be relevant to conduct of life.
    1. Youth—Prayer-books and devotions—English. [1. Prayer books and devotions. 2. Conducts of life] I. Dugan, LeRoy, ill. II. Ahlquist, Neil, ill. III. Title. IV. Series.
BV4850.P45   248.8'3   81-38465
ISBN 0-87123-167-0 (pbk.)   AACR2

About the Author

LORRAINE PETERSON was born in Red Wing, Minnesota, grew up on a farm near Ellsworth, Wisconsin, and now is teaching in Mexico. She received her B.A. (in history) from North Park College in Chicago, and has taken summer courses from the University of Minnesota and the University of Mexico in Mexico City.

Lorraine has taught high school and junior high. She has been an advisor to nondenominational Christian clubs in Minneapolis public schools and has taught teenage Bible studies. Her first book is the bestseller, *If God Loves Me, Why Can't I Get My Locker Open?*

Preface

As a teenager, you no doubt ask a lot of searching questions and do a lot of deep thinking. The aim of this book is to address some of your concerns and to present spiritual truth in a way that is relevant to your life.

God's Word can be living and active only as it is daily studied and applied in real-life situations. My prayer is that this book will help you establish a daily quiet time with God.

I have been greatly influenced by the writings of Watchman Nee and Andrew Murray. I have also used ideas from Bill Gothard's Basic Youth Conflicts seminar, Mel Johnson's "Tips for Teens" radio program, and a book by Robert Mattox entitled *The Christian Employee.*

I have weekly benefited from sermons given by Pastor Ernest O'Neill of Campus Church, Sunday school lessons taught by Leighton Carlson, and a Tuesday night Bible study led by Michael O'Connor. These three men will recognize some of their thoughts and illustrations in this book. These men have obeyed Paul's command that says, "And what you have heard . . . entrust to faithful men who will be able to teach others also" (2 Tim. 2:2).

I'd like to express my appreciation to several people. My patient and long-suffering roommates, Karen, Kris, and Laurie, have discovered that living with an author means a messy dining room table. My father, my sister, my brother-in-law, and my nieces and nephews, Beth, Brett, Kaari, and Kirk, encouraged and tolerated a recluse during much of my Christmas vacation. My Aunt Harriet provided her upstairs as a quiet place to write—complete with room service and excellent meals—so that I could finish this manuscript on time.

The illustrations in this book are based on sketches made by Neil Ahlquist when he was still a high school student. He willingly made dozens of drawings for my Bible study lessons when writing a book was still only a dream.

It is to Neil and the many other students with whom I worked at Edison High School and Northeast Junior High that I express my deepest gratitude. The questions they asked me and the things they shared with me were the inspiration for this book.

Table of Contents

How to Use This Book

To teenagers for daily devotions: In order to get the most out of these lessons, keep a notebook and *write down* the answers. The lazy part of you is saying, "I don't want to—it's too much work." However, education research supports the idea that you remember things you write down longer than things you only think about. God's Word is very important—important enough to get your best effort.

To youth workers for Sunday school or Bible study material: Leaders should assign the daily readings for the week. Ask students to write out the answers to the questions along with any new questions which they would like to discuss with the group. The leader can pick out the most important questions and ask members to contribute their findings. If it is not practical for your group to prepare in advance, it would be better to spend at least two weeks on each topic, read the material in class, and cover the questions as you go along. The teacher will want to add questions and thoughts which are specifically relevant to the particular group being taught.

Week One

THE MOST IMPORTANT BOOK IN THE WORLD

The Riches You Could Have

I once heard a story about a Texas family who saved and scrimped, going without many things in order to pay off the mortgage on their farm. All the while these people were ignorant of one fact: *there was oil under their land.* Lack of knowledge condemned them to poverty.

Of course, even after discovering oil, those people could have chosen to ignore this resource and remain poor. Many people treat the promises in God's Word the same way. Although they know the promises, they refuse to act upon them, and their lives remain unchanged. They want to have their lives changed, but they doubt whether God would really do such good things for them.

Unlike people, God doesn't promise anything He is unable or unwilling to give or do. He doesn't resent being reminded of His promises. In fact, when you claim one of His promises, He *loves* it!

We often get into trouble when we pray because, being ignorant of God's promises, we ask for things God has never promised to give. For example, if a kind rich man promised to send a poor boy to an expensive private school, would the boy be justified in complaining that the rich man hadn't bought him a ten-speed or given him a free trip to Disney World? Obviously the man could be held responsible only for what he had *promised* to give the boy. We need to remember that God didn't promise sunshine for all our picnics, but He did promise to give us peace "which passes all understanding" (Phil. 4:7).

Claim a promise from God's Word. Stick with that promise and keep asking God to make it real in your life.

"God is not man, that he should lie, or a son of man, that he should repent. Has he said, and will he not do it? Or has he spoken, and will he not fulfil it?" (Num. 23:19).

"Since we have these promises, beloved, let us cleanse ourselves from every defilement of body and spirit, and make holiness perfect in the fear of God" (2 Cor. 7:1).

1. Why are God's promises different from men's promises?

14

2. How should *your* life be different because of the promises God has given?
3. As you read in your Bible today, find one promise and claim it for your life.

What You Don't Know Can Hurt You

I'll always remember one Saturday morning. I got up early to attend a Bible study. I'd gone to church all my life and thought I knew my Bible pretty well. But we studied the first chapter of Ephesians, and I learned for the first time that the power of the Holy Spirit within me is the same power that raised Jesus from the dead. Wow! That's a lot of power! I could never again say that I was powerless to do what God asked of me. I had within me the power that raised Jesus from the dead. That Bible truth has made a big difference in my life.

The Bible is full of spiritual principles which the Holy Spirit wants to apply to our lives. How many people have to look back on their lives and sadly say, "If I had only known and applied what the Bible teaches, this would not have happened to me."

An increasing knowledge of God's Word and a deeper obedience to God's commands will assure you of an abundant and joyful life. The Bible is like a huge gold mine—you'll always keep finding more treasure if you're willing to search for it. But what you don't know about the Bible can hurt you.

"My people are destroyed for lack of knowledge; because you have rejected knowledge, I reject you from being a priest to me. And since you have forgotten the law of your God, I also will forget your children" (Hos. 4:6).

"While they were bringing out the money that had been brought into the house of the Lord, Hilkiah the priest found the book of the law of the Lord given through Moses. . . . And Shaphan read it before the king. When the king heard the words of the law he rent his clothes. [He tore them as a sign of great sorrow and distress.] And

15

the king commanded . . . 'Go, inquire of the Lord for me and for those who are left in Israel and in Judah, concerning the words of the book that has been found; for great is the wrath of the Lord that is poured out on us, because our fathers have not kept the word of the Lord, to do according to all that is written in this book' " (2 Chron. 34:14, 18-21).

1. What are the consequences of being ignorant of God's Word?
2. Why was the king so upset that he tore his clothes?
3. Do you become distressed when you discover that something in your life is not pleasing to God? If your answer is "no," why?

Hearing God's Word

Suppose Jesus came in person and spoke to your church, youth group, or Bible study club. Would you daydream through His talk, fall asleep, whisper to your friends, or try to get the attention of your buddy across the room? I don't think so. But have you ever realized that since God is the author of the Bible, each of us has a tremendous responsibility each time we hear it read and explained? How you *hear* the Word of God can determine whether you go to heaven or hell, whether you will follow Jesus or not.

Inattentiveness to God's Word can ruin your life. The devil knows this and will try to make you think that goofing around or daydreaming during a Bible study or keeping someone else from listening to a scripture lesson is innocent fun. It isn't.

Really listening isn't easy; neither is concentrating when you read the Bible for yourself. You will need God's help. Confess any wrong attitudes you may have in this area and ask God to show you how to change. Don't ever come to a meeting thinking, "This is easy. All I have to do is sit and listen." Pray for God's help each time you are to listen to His Word. Make up your mind to listen attentively every time you hear a scripture reading, a sermon, or a Bible talk. Take notes—even if no one else does—to help you concentrate. When you study the Bible for yourself, decide to get everything possible out of it. Really hearing God's Word will be, like so many hard things, completely worthwhile.

"And the word which you hear is not mine but the Father's who sent me" (John 14:24).

"You have neither listened nor inclined your ears to hear, although the Lord persistently sent to you all his servants the prophets, saying, 'Turn now, every one of you, from his evil way and wrong doings, and dwell upon the land which the Lord has given to you and your fathers. . . .' Yet you have not listened to me, says the Lord, that you might provoke me to anger with the work of your hands to your own harm. Therefore thus says the Lord of hosts: Because you have not obeyed my words. . . . This whole land shall become a ruin and a waste, and these nations shall serve the king of Babylon seventy years" (Jer. 25:4, 5, 7, 8, 11).

1. Why was God forced to punish and judge the people of ancient Judah?
2. How could the people have avoided God's judgment?
3. What problems can be prevented in your life if you listen to and obey God's Word?

"But I Thought You Said 'Hit It' "

The Word of God contains truths that will give you an abundant and joyful life—IF you hear them, understand them, and apply them. Doing this is a little bit like eating a meal. You aren't ready for more food until you've at least partially digested what you last put into your mouth. If you listen carefully and obey God's Word, it will become part of you, and you will be ready to receive more. The person who takes a flippant attitude toward the Bible will eventually lose any "faith" he or she might have had.

God expects us to listen to Him attentively and obey exactly. Moses once hit a rock instead of speaking to it as God had commanded. As punishment he was not allowed to enter the land God promised His people, the land that was the goal of Moses and his people for forty years. Whether Moses thought that giving the rock a couple whacks with his rod would help God get water from a rock, whether he was letting out his frustration because the people were

17

getting on his nerves, or whether he never listened carefully in the first place, we are not told. However, the story shows that God expects us to listen to His Word so attentively that we can obey it exactly. Listening is an art. Ask God to help you listen better to His Word and to listen more carefully to your parents, teachers, and friends.

"And the Lord said to Moses, 'Take the rod and assemble the congregation, you and Aaron your brother, and tell the rock before their eyes to yield its water; so you shall bring water out of the rock for them; so you shall give drink to the congregation and their cattle.' And Moses took the rod from before the Lord, as he commanded him. And Moses and Aaron gathered the assembly together before the rock and he said to them, 'Hear now, you rebels; shall we bring forth water for you out of this rock?' And Moses lifted up his hand and struck the rock with his rod twice; and water came forth abundantly, and the congregation drank, and their cattle. And the Lord said to Moses and Aaron, 'Because you did not believe in me, to sanctify me in the eyes of the people of Israel, therefore you shall not bring this assembly into the land which I have given them'" (Num. 20:7-12).

"Take heed then how you hear; for to him who has will more be given, and from him who has not, even what he thinks that he has will be taken away" (Luke 8:18).

1. Why do *you* think Moses hit the rock instead of speaking to it?
2. Why do you think God considers following His instructions such a serious matter?
3. Are there any of God's instructions that you aren't obeying? Which one should you start working on first?

Second Helpings for Hungry Hearts

Your spiritual growth will depend, in large measure, on how you "eat" the Word of God. It is spiritual food, and a malnourished Christian, one who neglects that food, will certainly be weak. It's not the quantity of food on the *table* but the quantity that gets *inside* you which is important.

If the Bible is to really become a part of you, it is necessary to remember that your *heart* is more important than your *mind* when you are studying the Bible. With your mind you understand and comprehend but with your heart you desire, love, and hold fast to Jesus. *Your mind must be the servant of your heart.* You have given your *heart* to Jesus because He is the Son of God, He is truth, and He knows everything. The little bucket of your mind will not be able to contain the ocean of God's truth.

Spiritual truth is different from *intellectual* truth. It's not I.Q. but dedication to God which makes spiritual truth clear. Even in our human relationships, our hearts' sense of love and compassion is more important than intellectual understanding of every action and statement. Use your mind but remember that Bible study is not an intellectual exercise—it's fellowship with the living God. Let Him speak to you very personally and intimately through His living Word. If your heart is always hungry for more of God's truth, Bible study will be a real feast.

"With my whole heart I seek thee; let me not wander from thy commandments" (Ps. 119:10).

"But, as it is written, 'What no eye hath seen, nor ear heard, nor the heart of man conceived, what God has prepared for those who love him,' God has revealed to us through the Spirit. For the Spirit searches everything, even the depths of God. For what person knows a man's thoughts except the spirit of the man which is in him? So also no one comprehends the thoughts of God except the Spirit of God. Now we have received not the spirit of the world, but the Spirit which is from God, that we might understand the gifts bestowed on us by God. And we impart this in words not taught by human wisdom but taught by the Spirit, interpreting spiritual truths to those who possess the Spirit" (1 Cor. 2:9-13).

1. Who is the only One who can understand God's words and thoughts and interpret them to us?
2. Why is it wrong to try to figure out God's Word only by your intellect?
3. Do you pray for the guidance of the Holy Spirit as you read the Bible or do you depend on your intelligence?

Bible "Pit Stops"

Do you approach Bible study as a sort of "pit stop"? As you study, do you anxiously note the precious time used, then rejoin the rat race to finish all the things you need to do? If you use the "once over lightly" method of Bible study, God's Word will never become part of you and will never change your life.

God's Word needs and deserves a lot of your time. Skip your Thursday night TV shows or stay home from the basketball game to spend unhurried time in Bible study. Give God's living and powerful Word time to grow and mature in you. Be willing to search the Scriptures for answers to various questions. If a verse is unclear or confusing to you, be willing to look up all the verses on that topic.

When you ask a Bible scholar for an opinion, always ask for the scripture behind his opinion and study that scripture for yourself. Trust God for answers to the things in the Bible which you don't understand. If you diligently search the Scriptures, God will teach you the things you really must understand when you need to know them. If you, like Jeremiah, take the time to study God's words, digest them, and let them become a part of you, those words will make a drastic difference in your life.

"Thy words were found, and I ate them, and thy words became to me a joy and the delight of my heart; for I am called by thy name, O Lord, God of hosts" (Jer. 15:16).

"And these words which I command you this day shall be upon your heart; and you shall teach them diligently to your children, and shall talk of them when you sit in your house, and when you walk by the way, and when you lie down, and when you rise" (Deut. 6:6, 7).

"Oh, how I love thy law! It is my meditation all the day" (Ps. 119:97).

1. What attitudes toward Bible study are mentioned in these verses?
2. Why were the Israelites commanded to study and memorize the Bible constantly?
3. Why is it necessary for you to study the Bible continually?

Seeds Need Time to Grow

Have you ever opened your Bible, read a few verses and closed it again without feeling or learning anything? Then you hear the devil whisper, "You might as well quit reading the Bible. You don't get anything out of it anyway."

When this happens to you (and it will), don't get discouraged. When you start your Bible study, do you *pray in faith* asking the Holy Spirit to teach you from His Word? God honors faith. Someone has said, "If you expect nothing, you'll get it every time."

Also remember that studying the Bible is *hard work*. You sometimes need to do quite a bit of prospecting before you find gold. You may read a whole chapter or more before you come to the verse that the Holy Spirit wants to apply to your life for that day.

The most important thing to keep in mind is that seeds need time to grow. Suppose your neighbor said, "I planted my garden last night and it looks exactly the same this morning. It doesn't do any good to plant seeds." You would quickly tell him that he should wait longer.

In Luke 8:11 we read, "The seed is the word of God." We all

know that seed has to be planted in good soil. Reading and memorizing God's Word as well as meditating on it is like planting seed. If you sincerely desire to see God work in your life, the time you spend in Bible study is never wasted. It's like planting a seed. It may take time but it will grow. Your *attitude* determines the kind of soil the seed of God's Word has to grow in. Don't just read the Bible, meditate on it. Obey it and live by it. Keep it with you all through the day, and it will work in you.

"Therefore put away all filthiness and rank growth of wickedness and receive with meekness the implanted word which is able to save your souls" (James 1:21).

"For as the rain and the snow come down from heaven, and return not thither but water the earth, making it bring forth and sprout, giving seed to the sower and bread to the eater, so shall my word be that goes forth from my mouth; it shall not return to me empty, but it shall accomplish that which I purpose and prosper in the thing for which I sent it" (Isa. 55:10, 11).

1. What do you learn about God's Word from these verses?
2. Notice that God doesn't say that His Word will accomplish His purpose instantly, or in a week, or in ten days. Have you ever put time limits on God?
3. Are you willing to carefully study God's Word and give it time to grow in your life?

Week Two

OBEY IS A FOUR-LETTER WORD

God's Word in Your Heart

When you fall in love, you cherish the words of the person you love. Those words change you as you contemplate the comforting thought that one person loves you and will stick with you no matter what.

After a parent has died, the children still remember his words of advice and often allow that advice to direct their lives.

The problem is that there are limits on the power of human words. The person who has stated, "I'll love you forever," may forget that promise within a month and the once-comforting words become painful memories. Parents can give wrong advice and the changes this advice makes in the lives of their children may be devastating.

God's Word is different. It is *always* true, *always* reliable, and *always* the best advice. Do you have the kind of love relationship with God that makes His words all-important to you? Do you ponder the verses you read, keep them in your heart, and think about them all day long? If hearing God's words is only an intellectual exercise, your life won't change. But if God's words reach your heart so that you cherish them and determine to obey them, God will use His words to transform your life.

"With my whole heart I seek thee; let me not wander from thy commandments! I have laid up thy word in my heart that I might not sin against thee" (Ps. 119:10, 11).

"Let thy steadfast love come to me, O Lord, thy salvation according to thy promise; then shall I have an answer for those who taunt me, for I trust in thy word. And take not the word of truth utterly out of my mouth, for my hope is in thy ordinances. I will keep thy law continually, for ever and ever; and I shall walk at liberty, for I have sought thy precepts. I will also speak of thy testimonies before kings, and shall not be put to shame; for I find my delight in thy commandments, which I love. I revere [regard with deep respect] *thy commandments which I love, and I will meditate on thy statutes"* (Ps. 119:41-49).

1. List all the things which characterize the Psalmist's attitude toward God's Word.

2. What things will believing and acting on God's Word do for a person?
3. Which of these things do you need most right now? Ask God to fulfill this need as you study His Word.

You Know—or Do You?

Perhaps you've seen a cartoon character with a light bulb on top of his head, symbolizing a moment of illumination. Sometimes you feel like that. Something you knew as a fact suddenly becomes part of your experience. Maybe you knew the fact that Jesus saves long before it became real to you through accepting Jesus as your own personal Savior. Knowledge was the first step, because if you had no idea that Jesus could save you, you wouldn't have thought of giving your life to Him. But acting on God's truth turned information into reality.

Imagine a beautiful castle and a fantastic yard, surrounded by a high wall with only one gate. Rumor has it that lions live in this yard, and getting into the castle itself is impossible for anyone. As you walk along the road one day, you pick up a piece of paper with these words: "To the reader of this letter: If you come to the gate at midnight, it will be opened and you will be safely received. If you wait by the castle door until it is opened, you will become my heir."

Understanding the instructions would make it possible for you to get into the yard. However, it would take great faith if you had to wait by the castle door for three days without food, in cold and rainy weather, for the owner to open the door and finally let you experience all his riches. There's also a big difference between believing God's Word intellectually and having enough faith to act on it, particularly if the action is difficult, if your friends think you're crazy, or if it seems contrary to reason.

"Thy word is a lamp to my feet and a light to my path" (Ps. 119:105).

"But the word is very near you; it is in your mouth and in your heart, so that you can do it" (Deut. 30:14).

"I will run in the way of thy commandments when thou enlarg-

est my understanding! Teach me, O Lord, the way of thy statutes; and I will keep it to the end. Give me understanding, that I may keep thy law and observe it with my whole heart" (Ps. 119:32-34).

1. In Psalm 119:105, what is God's Word compared to? (Light has different intensities. Each Bible passage sheds light for the person sincerely studying it. Restudying, memorizing, and obeying are like turning up the voltage and receiving more illumination.)
2. In Deuteronomy 30:14, what are the stages for God's Word to really become part of you?
3. What attitudes toward God's Word do you see in Psalm 119:32-34?

Powerful Stuff

Bible study is not necessarily pleasant. The old expression "The truth hurts" has real validity. Honestly facing ourselves and being willing to change is not easy, but earnest Bible study requires us to do just that.

Often God's words don't "get through" to us because we rationalize. We take God's Word and try to soften its impact with our own reasoning. The Bible may say, "Be still and know that I am God," but our reasoning says, "That's okay for Old Testament shepherds, but things are so bad for me I have to do something—run away from home, drop out of school, get married—anything to get out of this mess."

When we use our own reasoning, the Bible becomes nothing more than a book to study, and its power to change our lives is useless. Others, like the Pharisees of Jesus' day, have added things from their own culture or their own personalities, distorting its true meaning. Because of this, it is very important to ask the Holy Spirit to help you interpret the Bible. Only the Holy Spirit can help you apply the truths of the Bible to everyday life.

All of us approach the Bible with a lot of preconceived ideas and misinformation. We hear this axiom, "You've got to work for what you get," so often that we easily get caught up in earning our way to heaven or winning God's approval. No doubt you've also heard

"God helps those who help themselves" so often you think it's a Bible verse. It isn't. From this statement we get the false idea that asking God's help should be a last resort—after everything else has been tried. We must approach God's Word as little children who know nothing and who expect it to change all our attitudes and all our actions. When we let the Bible speak to us and remake us, God's Word is powerful stuff.

"For the word of God is living and active, sharper than any two-edged sword, piercing to the division of soul and spirit, of joints and marrow, and discerning the thoughts and intentions of the heart. And before him no creature is hidden, but all are open and laid bare

to the eyes of him with whom we have to do" (Heb. 4:12, 13).

" 'The grass withers, and the flower falls, but the word of the Lord abides for ever.' That word is the good news which was preached to you. So put away all malice [bad intentions] and all guile [deceitfulness] and insincerity and envy and all slander. Like newborn babes, long for the pure spiritual milk, that by it you may grow up to salvation" (1 Pet. 1:24, 25; 2:1, 2).

1. What qualities of God's Word are mentioned in the previous verses?
2. With what attitudes are we to approach the study of the Bible?
3. What attitudes toward Bible study do you have which need to be improved?

Alarm Clocks and God's Promises

Have you ever considered that God invented morning and may not appreciate your complaints about it? How do you start each day? Do you growl at your alarm clock and feel like tossing it out the window? Do you give your mother a rough time when she admonishes you to get up? Is your first thought of every day, "Oh, no, do I have to get up?"

You could, instead, start the new day by thanking Jesus for the new life He has put within you, for giving you victory in your life for that day. You don't have to be a saintly super-Christian to have this kind of faith to start each day. The Word of God can bring you the faith you do not have. The Bible is living and powerful; it will *work* in you.

Keep thinking about one of God's promises during the day. For example, the Bible says, "This is the day which the Lord has made; let us rejoice and be glad in it" (Ps. 118:24). You may not feel one bit like rejoicing or thanking God for the day. However, the Word of God is *living*. Believe it and hang on to it. Let God's Word give you faith for strength and obedience.

Practice this each morning for a month—then for the rest of your life. As soon as you wake up, say to yourself, " 'This is the day which the Lord has made; let us rejoice and be glad in it.' Lord, I thank you for this day." If you claim this verse with real faith in God, it's no longer just positive thinking. It's linking yourself up with God and making it possible for Him to work a miracle in your life.

God *can* change your attitude toward morning if you are willing to cooperate with Him. Cooperation not only includes practicing God's promises but also means doing common-sense things such as not staying out later than you should. A racer always makes sure of a good start or there is no chance of winning. Shouldn't you let God's Word work in you to get you off to a winning start each day?

"It is the spirit that gives life, the flesh is of no avail; the words that I have spoken to you are spirit and life" (John 6:63).

"And we also thank God constantly for this, that when you received the word of God which you heard from us, you accepted it not as the word of men but as what it really is, the word of God, which is at work in you believers" (1 Thess. 2:13).

1. What will we accomplish by doing things "in the flesh" (without God's help)?
2. Why do you think God's words are "spirit and life"?
3. Will you give God's Word a chance to work in your life? In what specific area do you need God's special help? Ask Him for guidance and for scripture verses that will be of special help to you.

Walking Around Walls and Other Crazy Behavior

Obedience makes Bible study exciting! Reading directions about how to assemble a jet engine is sheer boredom unless you're building a plane. Then the directions make interesting reading.

The Bible says things like "Obey your parents" and "Honor all men." These commandments are just words on a page unless you decide that you will obey God and believe Him for miracles in your life. Decide you will clean your room every time your mother tells you to. Ask God to give you the right attitude toward your mother and God will change your attitude. If you keep obeying your mother on this point and in faith expect God to change you, God can eliminate the friction between you and your mom and make you a better housekeeper.

When you realize that "Honor all men" includes your crabby chemistry teacher, "Mr. Formula," you will decide to resign from the committee which thinks up new names for him and plays jokes on him. If you speak respectfully to him at all times, and pray for him, you'll see God change your attitude toward that man.

Read the Bible intending to obey it or you'll miss out on all the good stuff—*miracles* in your very own life!

When Joshua received God's directions for defeating the city of Jericho, he didn't say, "My devotions this morning were especially interesting. By the way, would anybody like to go on a picnic?" or, "The Lord gave me some directions but His methods seem too old-fashioned. If we didn't have modern weapons, I could understand just trusting the Lord." Joshua *obeyed* God, and all the Israelites saw the walls of Jericho crumble before their eyes. Joshua believed God's Word was not only to be heard and read but also to be obeyed.

"Behold, I set before you this day a blessing and a curse: the blessing, if you obey the comandments of the Lord your God, which I command you this day, and the curse, if you do not obey the commandments of the Lord your God. . ." (Deut. 11:26-28).

"On the seventh day they rose early at the dawn of day, and marched around the city in the same manner seven times. . . . And at the seventh time, when the priests had blown the trumpets, Joshua said to the people, 'Shout; for the Lord has given you the city.' So the people shouted and the trumpets were blown. As soon as the people heard the sound of the trumpet, the people raised a great shout, and the wall fell down flat. . ." (Josh. 6:15, 16, 20).

1. Why do God's commandments become a curse to us if we refuse to obey them?
2. What do you think would have happened if Joshua would not have obeyed God?
3. What step of obedience does God want you to take today?

Know-It-All Christians and Steep Drop-offs

Are you a know-it-all Christian? Do you have the books of the Bible memorized backwards? Are you sick of hearing the same verses and the same material over and over again? Are you a right-answer computer bank? If you are, watch out! There's a steep cliff right around the corner and you're the most likely candidate to fall off it—just like the disciple who was so sure of himself but denied Jesus, not once, but three times in a row!

God's truth is constantly contradicted, so you must keep reviewing it to counteract all the things the world is telling you. After four TV commercials telling you that you can't exist without a certain new car, that you're ugly without this suntan lotion, that you haven't lived unless you've seen the latest movie, and that all the important people are vacationing in Hawaii, you probably need to read the words, "Seek ye first the kingdom of God" (Matt. 6:33, KJV) many times.

The new life which Jesus gave you when you accepted Him is not to be understood in human terms. Ignorance of spiritual principles can keep you from growing as a Christian, and the devil is working overtime to keep you ignorant of the truth which can give you victory.

Ignorance of the dangers of plugging in a wet extension cord, or of driving a snowmobile over a partially frozen lake, or of lighting a match too close to a gasoline tank can cause serious consequences. In the same way ignorance of the laws of the spiritual life can get you into a lot of trouble. You need to study the Bible carefully to learn more of God's truth. All of us need to approach the Christian life admitting that we are ignorant of God's ways and that we have *everything* to learn. It does stand to reason that God is smarter than we are.

" 'For my thoughts are not your thoughts, neither are your ways my ways, says the Lord. For as the heavens are higher than the earth, so are my ways higher than your ways and my thoughts than your thoughts' " (Isa. 55:8, 9).

"Lead me in thy truth, and teach me, for thou art the God of my salvation; for thee I wait all the day long. Good and upright is the

Lord; therefore he instructs sinners in the way. He leads the humble in what is right, and teaches the humble his way" (Ps. 25:5, 8, 9).

1. With what attitudes should we approach Bible study?
2. Do you study the Bible to learn facts or to let God show you how to live your life?

Not Just for Wall Plaques

There is no magic in just reading the Bible and knowing what it says. The boy who wins the Old Testament Quiz Contest is not necessarily the best Christian. The girl who memorizes the most verses and wins the bike in the Vacation Bible School competition isn't automatically spiritual. People can read the Bible every day without it making a dent in the way they live.

Some who are familiar with the contents of the Bible consider studying it rather boring. On the other hand, George Mueller who prayed in money to feed and clothe thousands of orphans read through the Bible one hundred times and found it more precious and exciting each time.

What's the difference? You can't read the words of Jesus carefully without noticing that they are commandments to be obeyed and not just words to put on wall plaques. Just knowing the Word of God is not enough. Demons, atheists, alcoholics, liars and swindlers often know it also. *Obeying* God's Word is what counts.

You could memorize directions on how to make a dress or how to tune up a car, but they will have little significance until they are put into practice. You put God's Word "into practice" by obeying it. Either you obey and the meaning of His instructions become clear and more beautiful or you disobey, harden your heart, and become more confused. The Bible says that obedience is better than sacrifice. It's also better than studying the original Greek, collecting dozens of cross references, buying memory verse packs, and underlining your Bible in pink, purple, and turquoise!

Studying God's Word diligently and carefully can never, never replace obedience. Hearing or reading God's Word can actually be dangerous—if you have already decided you won't obey God. It will only make you harder. But approaching God's Word with an open mind, a loving heart, and a willingness to obey is one of the most beautiful experiences on earth.

" 'Today, when you hear his voice, do not harden your hearts' " (Heb. 4:7).

"But be doers of the word, and not hearers only, deceiving yourselves. For if any one is a hearer of the word and not a doer, he is like a man who observes his natural face in a mirror; for he observes himself and goes away and at once forgets what he was like. But he who looks into the perfect law, the law of liberty, and perseveres, being no hearer that forgets but a doer that acts, he shall be blessed in his doing" (James 1:22-25).

1. What is your natural impulse when you look in a mirror?
2. Why is it easy to forget our image as soon as we leave the mirror?
3. Why is God's Word like a mirror and what should happen to us when we read it?

Week Three

FAITH IS NOT A BLIND LEAP

Jumping Out of Windows

I have "faith" that the sky will turn pink! I "believe" I'll live to be 95. I have "faith" that Russia will be a weak country in five years. Sounds ridiculous, doesn't it? What is faith, anyway?

The faith of a Christian always attaches itself to what God has promised. A trustworthy person keeps his or her word. God is trustworthy. He never makes a promise He will not keep. A three-year-old who trusts his father will jump out of a window into his father's waiting arms. But the promise, "I'll catch you if you jump" means nothing if the child refuses to jump.

Faith is an absolute certainty that what God says is true. Obviously, if you don't know exactly what God says, you can't have real faith. The statement, "I have faith that everything will turn out okay," is usually a bluff—revealing ignorance of God's Word. Study God's Word carefully. Hang onto what He has promised and be willing to jump into His waiting arms. If God doesn't tell you to do a dangerous or unusual thing and you do it anyway, don't blame Him for the consequences. Since faith is rooted in believing what God says, a "blind leap" has nothing to do with God or with faith.

God promises, I believe, and God fulfills. That is the secret of the life of faith.

"Not one of all the good promises which the Lord had made to the house of Israel had failed; all came to pass" (Josh. 21:45).

"Now the Lord said to Abram, 'Go from your country and your kindred [relatives] and your father's house to the land that I will show you. And I will make of you a great nation, and I will bless you, and make your name great, so that you will be a blessing. I will bless those who bless you, and him who curses you I will curse; and by you all the families of the earth shall bless themselves.' So Abram went, as the Lord had told him; and Lot went with him. Abram was seventy-five years old when he departed from Haran. And Abram took Sarai his wife, and Lot his brother's son, and all their possessions which they had gathered, and the persons that they had gotten in Haran; and they set forth to go to the land of Canaan" (Gen. 12:1-5).

1. Why was Abram's move to Canaan a step of faith?

2. If you just decide on the spur of the moment to hitchhike across the country because you have nothing better to do, are you exercising faith in God?

3. What things are you now doing because you know God wants you to do them? Are there projects and activities you are engaged in that you have never discussed with God? Ask God to show you what to do so that you can live by faith.

Decisions and Emotions

A lady who found herself in a very difficult situation went to a friend for advice. As she explained the problem she cried, "But I don't understand!"

Her friend replied, "At a time like this, you don't need to understand. You need to *trust*. Trusting God is not a feeling. It's a *decision*."

Do you ever try to gauge your faith by how you feel? Do you say, "I don't even have butterflies in my stomach before the game so I must be trusting God more"? Or do you feel that you must not be trusting God because you're scared to fly in an airplane? Do you think that the person who doesn't cry at a funeral trusts God more than you do? The truth is, that our emotions can be kept under control, even if we aren't exercising faith in God.

Whether or not you trust God depends on your *decision*, not on your emotions. For example, let's say that you have been dating a non-Christian and you know you shouldn't. Besides the fact that you really care about this person, you feel that there's no one else around you would ever date. In this case, you are not trusting God with your social life or with the life of the other person. If you decide to break off this relationship and to trust God with your dating life and the other person's emotions, you may feel worse after you made the decision than before. But keep trusting God.

You may have to pray ten times a day, "God, I give my friend to you and know that you can help my friend more than I ever could. I give my dating life and my emotions to you." Your decision to trust God will eventually bring your feelings into line, though this may take time. Your decision to trust God rather than your emotions is the all important thing.

"*For God alone my soul waits in silence; from him comes my salvation. He only is my rock and my salvation, my fortress; I shall not be greatly moved. How long will you set upon a man to shatter him, all of you, like a leaning wall, a tottering fence? They only plan to thrust him down from his eminence. They take pleasure in falsehood. They bless with their mouths, but inwardly they curse. For God alone my soul waits in silence, for my hope is from him. He only is my rock and my salvation, my fortress; I shall not be shaken. On God rests my deliverance and my honor; my mighty rock, my refuge is God. Trust in him at all times, O people; pour out your heart before him; God is a refuge for us*"* (Ps. 62:1-8).

"*Trust in the Lord with all your heart, and do not rely on your own insight*" (Prov. 3:5).

1. What are all the things God can be for us?
2. What problems and emotions are the writer of the Psalms struggling with?
3. Why should you rely on God rather than your insight?

His Sheep Am I

Shepherds in the Middle East still herd their sheep as their ancestors did centuries ago. A good shepherd loves each one of his sheep, giving protection, discipline, and direction. Sheep learn to follow their shepherd with an attitude of trust. To the extent that sheep are capable of it, there is a relationship of love and affection between the shepherd and his sheep.

The shepherd would do anything possible to protect and help the sheep. Recognizing this, the sheep obediently follow the shepherd.

However, there are things the shepherd must do which the sheep with their limited understanding cannot comprehend. There are beautiful hills which the sheep are never allowed to graze on—the owners of those hills would rather have mutton than wool! Because there are many diseases that the sheep could catch, modern shepherds sometimes find it necessary to completely submerge each sheep in an antiseptic solution. This process, which must take place regularly, is something the sheep hate and fear. Yet, it is impossible for the shepherd to explain to them why it is necessary.

Jesus, the Good Shepherd, also must take you through hard things which you with your limited understanding cannot figure out. However, if you take the time to get to know Jesus, you will have the certainty that He is the source of all good and all wisdom, and you'll want to follow Him anywhere. It's wonderful to follow Someone who knows in all cases what is best for you.

" 'I am the good shepherd. The good shepherd lays down his life for the sheep. He who is a hireling [paid employee] and not a shepherd, whose own the sheep are not, sees the wolf coming and leaves the sheep and flees; and the wolf snatches them and scatters them. He flees because he is a hireling and cares nothing for the sheep. I am the good shepherd; I know my own and my own know me, as the Father knows me and I know the Father; and I lay down my life for the sheep' " (John 10:11-15).

1. Why don't you have to be afraid to follow Jesus?
2. Have you had experiences with people who tried to take advantage of you? Ask Jesus to heal the hurt from these experiences.

why shouldn't these hurts from your past keep you from trusting Jesus?

3. Thank Jesus for being your Good Shepherd.

Feelings and Faith

Do thoughts like these keep passing through your mind? "I don't particularly feel like going to church this morning." "I feel more like going swimming than reading the Bible." "I don't feel like my prayers are getting through." "The thought of my sacrificing something so that people in Nepal can hear about Jesus leaves me cold." "I don't feel as if I am making any progress in the Christian life." "I don't feel like a joyful Christian tonight."

Someone has said, "Feelings are like the weather—subject to change." Although you may know that being a Christian depends on faith and not on feeling, like many people you may start depending on your feelings for living the Christian life. Emotions and feelings are very unpredictable. God is not. The Bible is just as true if you fall asleep reading it as it is if you sit on the edge of your chair wondering what Joshua will do next.

Obey God whether or not you feel like it. Have you ever been especially blessed by a church service you didn't feel like attending? Have you ever opened your Bible while your mind was busily planning an afternoon at the beach, but in spite of everything God spoke to you? Have you ever found that the lonely person you didn't really want to take the time to help actually made your day? Most of us can answer "yes" to these questions and can realize that living by our feelings is wrong.

Let faith speak out against your feelings. When feeling says, "In myself I am sinful, depressed, weak, poor, and sad," let faith answer, "In Christ I am holy, lighthearted, strong, rich, and joyful!" When you step out in faith, sooner or later the right feelings will catch up with you.

"And when he had ceased speaking, he said to Simon, 'Put out into the deep and let down your nets for a catch.' And Simon answered, 'Master, we toiled all night and took nothing! But at your word I will let down the nets.' And when they had done this, they

40

enclosed a great shoal of fish; and as their nets were breaking, they beckoned to their partners in the other boat to come and help them. And they came and filled both the boats, so that they began to sink" (Luke 5:4-7).
"For we walk by faith, not by sight" (2 Cor. 5:7).

1. After fishing all night and catching nothing, how do you suppose Peter *felt* about the command, "Put out into the deep and let down your nets for a catch"?
2. What were the results of Peter's faith and obedience (long-term and short-term)? How might history have been different if Peter had followed his feelings? (Read Acts 2 and Acts 10.)
3. Are you willing to obey the voice of Jesus regardless of your feelings? Is there anything Jesus is asking you to do now that you don't feel like doing?

If God Really Bats a Thousand, Why Do You Use Him Only as a Pinch Hitter?

As you probably know, John D. Rockefeller was one of the richest people who ever lived. You may be surprised to learn that he had a daughter who became obsessed with the fear that she would die penniless. The very thought of a Rockefeller being poor sounds ridiculous to one who knows anything about the family's fortune. Although a person may have wanted to feel sorry for this woman, he would have had to admit that her state of mind was caused by a stubborn refusal to believe provable facts.

A passage in the Psalms tells us that the Israelites who had seen God open the Red Sea were unwilling to trust Him for their daily needs in the wilderness: "They tested him again and again, and provoked the Holy One of Israel. They did not keep in mind his power, or the day when he redeemed them from the foe" (Ps. 78:41, 42).

God always has enough power to deliver us and will work miracles in response to our faith. He bats a thousand. Only our stubbornness prevents Him from working out our problems. That stub-

41

bornness comes in containers marked: "I just can't take it any longer," "This isn't fair," "I have a right to a little self-pity," or, "God, why don't you pick on someone else?" Such lack of faith prevents God's miracles.

God has enough grace to enable you to cheerfully obey your boss—if you'll stop being stubborn about your rights; God has enough love to heal your broken heart—if you'll give up that feeling-sorry-for-yourself routine; and God has enough power to enable you to clean your room every week—if you're willing to obey your mother. Don't be too obstinate to live by faith. The Bible calls lack of faith sin.

"And the Lord said to Moses, 'How long will this people despise me? And how long will they not believe in me, in spite of all the signs which I have wrought among them?' " (Num. 14:11).

"Hearken to me, you stubborn of heart, you who are far from deliverance: I bring near my deliverance, it is not far off, and my salvation will not tarry" (Isa. 46:12, 13).

"For whatever does not proceed from faith is sin" (Rom. 14:23).

1. Why can't God deliver a person who stubbornly clings to his own ways?
2. Why is lack of faith sin?
3. What is the hard thing you are facing this week—your Canaan to conquer? Is there any stubbornness in you that keeps you from believing God for a miracle?

Roller-Coaster Rides and Christians

Is your Christian experience a little like riding a big roller coaster? Are the ups and downs just too much and is getting off the best part of the ride? Are you one day nearly walking on water only to be in the pits of despair the next day, wondering if God really exists? That is not God's will for you. The Bible says, "The path of the upright is a *level* highway" (Prov. 15:19).

When you look at the road of life before you, it may resemble a stretch of highway in the Austrian Alps. But God wants to fill in the valleys and level the mountains, making the way smooth for you as you trust Him. The valleys are caused by lack of faith in God. Why do you think your parents' last fight depressed you? Why do you think Sylvia's insults devastated you? It's because you didn't trust God for your parents or for your reputation.

The peaks that are so hard to descend from are also your creations. If you imagine yourself as the guy who will throw the fifty-yard touchdown pass to win the game, it's difficult to face that eleven-yard punt. If you've dreamed and dreamed of becoming homecoming queen, having no date for the game is really hard to take. Do you discuss your dreams and hopes with God so He can change them? He wants to replace your daydreams with reality faith. Do you read His Word and let Him teach you to trust Him in every problem? Only Jesus can make your path into a level highway.

"The way of the righteous is level; thou dost make smooth the path of the righteous" (Isa. 26:7).

"A voice cries: 'In the wilderness, prepare the way of the Lord, make straight in the desert a highway for our God. Every valley shall be lifted up, and every mountain and hill be made low; the uneven ground shall become level, and the rough places a plain. And the glory of the Lord shall be revealed, and all flesh shall see it together, for the mouth of the Lord has spoken' " (Isa. 40:3-5).

1. Who can keep your life from becoming one long roller-coaster ride?
2. God wants your life to be a level highway. What is your responsibility in this?
3. Which one of your "ups" or "downs" should you deal with first?

"I Can Do It Myself"

I had just met the young man. He was a new Christian with a lot of questions and opinions. As we were talking about trusting God, he commented: "But marriage is something you decide for yourself." He obviously didn't understand what it means to trust God.

We cannot trust God if we think we know what we need better

than He does. If you've decided you *must* get straight A's, you won't trust God and experience His peace when you see a big fat C on your report card. If you're sure that you *must* be a success, you won't allow God to teach you a needed lesson when you lose the class election. If you've chosen popularity as your goal, you won't follow Jesus when it will make you unpopular to do so.

Are you like the five-year-old learning to hit a baseball? His response to the father's careful instructions is usually something like, "I can do it all by myself. I already know how, Dad, look at me." Then to prove that he knows how he puts pressure on himself to hit every ball. Being unable to face his failure, he suggests shooting baskets.

The "Lord, I can do it myself" Christian ends up as a frustrated failure. He would find it so much easier to relax and pray with the Psalmist, "Teach me thy way, O Lord."

"Trust in the Lord, and do good; so you will dwell in the land, and enjoy security. Take delight in the Lord, and he will give you the desires of your heart. Commit your way to the Lord; trust in him and he will act. The steps of a man are from the Lord, and he establishes him in whose way he delights; though he fall, he shall not be cast headlong, for the Lord is the stay of his hand" (Ps. 37:3-5, 23, 24).

1. What makes us think that we can run our lives better than God can?
2. Is there anything you want so much that you refuse to even consider God's opinion in the matter? If this is the case, what promise do you miss out on?
3. Why don't you confess right now that you need God to run your life because you don't dare trust yourself?

Week Four

MOUNTAIN-MOVING LESSONS

Are You a Rebecca?

Do you try to work out God's plans for Him? There's one four-letter word that most of us hate because we don't really know how to trust God. That four-letter word is WAIT.

Rebecca didn't like to wait. She and her husband, Isaac, had twin sons, Esau and Jacob. God had told her before the twins were born that Jacob, the younger son, would become greater and more important than his older brother, Esau. When it looked as if Isaac were going to give a special traditional blessing to Esau, Rebecca did not trust that God's promise would come true anyway. She did not wait to see how the God who had made the universe would handle this apparent contradiction. She took things into her own hands and tricked her husband, by convincing Jacob to lie, just so he could receive the blessing instead of Esau.

The results were disastrous. Esau found out and wanted to kill his brother. Jacob had to run away from home.

God has something very important to say about trusting Him when we don't see how things are going to turn out: "Who among you fears the Lord and obeys the voice of his servant, who walks in darkness and has no light, yet trusts in the name of the Lord and relies upon his God? Behold, all you who kindle a fire, who set brands alight! Walk by the light of your fire, and by the brands which you have kindled! This shall you have from my hand: you shall lie down in torment" (Isa. 50:10, 11).

We are always trying to light our paths with fires we start, but they rage out of control. You don't have to butter up the boss so that he'll give you the raise you need so badly. Just trust God. You don't have to drop your books in front of every member of the football team to try to land a date for Saturday night. God might just know what's best for your social life, so trust Him. You don't have to lie to your parents so you can go on the church retreat. God can even handle that situation. Trusting God takes the strain, the pressure, and the torment out of life.

"Wait for the Lord; be strong and let your heart take courage; yea, wait for the Lord" (Ps. 27:14).

"Therefore the Lord waits to be gracious to you; therefore he exalts himself to show mercy to you. For the Lord is a God of justice; blessed are all those who wait for him" (Isa. 30:18).

"No eye has seen a God besides thee, who works for those who wait for him" (Isa. 64:4).

1. What promises are contained in these verses?
2. In what areas of your life are you trying to make your own arrangements rather than waiting for God to act? Ask God for forgiveness and yield these areas of your life to Him.

Walking on the Water

There's a book with the title, *If You Want to Walk on Water, You've Got to Get Out of the Boat.* This title gets to the heart of a great spiritual truth: if we stay in safe territory all the time and never launch out on faith, we'll never experience all that God can do for us.

As a Christian teacher in a public school, I felt God wanted me to teach a Roman history lesson on true Christianity and the resurrection of Jesus. These were part of Roman history so I would not be breaking any law prohibiting religion in the classroom.

Fifth-hour class was filled with rowdy and sarcastic boys, not to mention girls. I was painfully aware of my inadequacies as a teacher and my classroom control left something to be desired. And of course, if someone misunderstood I could have gotten into problems with the administration. In spite of all this, I obeyed God.

When I started speaking, my voice was trembling and the notes I had in my unsteady hand were shaking. Yet, immediately the students became quiet and they listened intently. The only comment afterwards was a nice one, "Well, now we shouldn't have to go to church this Sunday." I had just seen God work a miracle!

God doesn't always make it that easy once we start obeying Him, but, as I've been told, "God doesn't give dying grace unless you're dying." He doesn't give us His miraculous power unless we are willing to put ourselves into a position where we need it. Do you intend to spend the rest of your life in the comfortable, boring boat, or do you plan to walk on the water?

"And Peter answered him, 'Lord, if it is you, bid me come to you on the water.' He said, 'Come.' So Peter got out of the boat and

walked on the water and came to Jesus; but when he saw the wind, he was afraid, and beginning to sink he cried out, 'Lord, save me.' Jesus immediately reached out his hand and caught him, saying to him, 'O man of little faith, why did you doubt?' And when they got into the boat, the wind ceased. And those in the boat worshiped him, saying, 'Truly you are the Son of God!' " (Matt. 14:28-33).

1. Are there situations in your life in which you need "to get out of the boat"? What are they?
2. Once you've obeyed Jesus and stepped out on faith, how can you still get in trouble?
3. Looking at the waves and not at Jesus, as Peter did, will always cause you problems. What circumstances are turning your eyes from Jesus? Ask Jesus to help you look to Him.

Fear Is a Nobody

Fear arises in at least three different circumstances: emergency panic situations, long-term problems such as disastrous financial or family difficulties, and an uncertain future. God doesn't want the devil to paralyze you with fear. God can give you peace even when you've missed your last bus home. He can keep you calm if you trust Him with your parents' divorce, your sister's attitude, or your physical handicap.

Satan loves to exploit your fear of the unknown. Your unrestricted imagination can make you afraid that you'll flunk out of the college you haven't even entered, that you'll get fired from the job you haven't even applied for, or that you'll get cancer and die before you graduate from high school.

Satan also uses fear of the *spiritual* unknown. He tries to make us afraid of giving God everything. As we imagine ourselves in a Communist prison camp ready to be led before a firing squad, the devil whispers, "That's what happens to all people who give God everything." Even though the Bible and hundreds of Christian biographies prove otherwise, we're still dumb enough to believe it. We forget that God gives supernatural power to Christians in especially tough circumstances. Our part is to trust Him and expect that power.

48

God wants to free us from fear. Someone once said, "Fear knocked at the door. Faith answered. No one was there." Fear is a nobody.

"No man shall be able to stand before you all the days of your life; as I was with Moses, so I will be with you; I will not fail you, or forsake you" (Josh. 1:5).

"Be strong and of good courage, and do it. Fear not, be not dismayed; for the Lord God, even my God, is with you. He will not fail you or forsake you, until all the work for the service of the house of the Lord is finished" (1 Chron. 28:20).

"Fear not, for I am with you, be not dismayed, for I am your God; I will strengthen you, I will help you, I will uphold you with my victorious right hand" (Isa. 41:10).

1. What are you facing within the next month that is making you afraid?
2. Using the above verses, what do you think God would say about that fear if He decided to send you a telegram?

Eradicate the Panic Button

Do you get a sinking feeling in your stomach when you discover that you've just lost your keys? Do you break out in a cold sweat when you realize that there's a big biology test and you haven't even read the chapter? Do your knees knock when you give a report in front of the English class? Are you always pushing the panic button? When you panic you are saying, "God, you just can't take care of me. What on earth will I do?"

There are two kinds of fear. Fear which keeps you from crossing a busy street with your eyes closed, which keeps you from jumping out of a third-story window, and which at least sometimes keeps you from a horrible sunburn is God's protection. But most fear is not only harmful but also wrong. And God would not command us to "fear not" if He could not give us peace to replace fear.

As a Christian facing a tight situation, you have two choices: you can panic or pray in faith. It may take time for your emotions to catch on to the fact that your will has determined to pray and trust

God rather than to panic, but bring your fears immediately to God and ask Him to calm you.

Reaction to emergency is habitual. Habits are broken slowly, just as they are formed slowly. Decide to bring each panic situation to God. Ask for forgiveness if you go through an entire crisis without even thinking about God. After a while, you'll start forming the habit of praying rather than panicking; but it all starts with a decision to trust God in EVERY situation.

"In God, whose word I praise, in God I trust without a fear. What can flesh do to me?" (Ps. 56:4).

"And when he got into the boat, his disciples followed him. And behold, there arose a great storm on the sea, so that the boat was being swamped by the waves; but he was asleep. And they went and woke him, saying, 'Save, Lord; we are perishing.' And he said to them, 'Why are you afraid, O men of little faith?' Then he rose and rebuked the winds and the sea; and there was a great calm. And the men marveled, saying, 'What sort of man is this, that even winds and sea obey him?' " (Matt. 8:23-27).

1. Several of the disciples were seasoned fishermen, but they were afraid of the storm. How critical do you think the situation was?
2. If the storm was so bad, why did Jesus scold the disciples?
3. Why was Jesus more concerned about the disciples' faith than their circumstance?
4. Are you living as if it is a sin not to trust God?

How to Enjoy Being Shipwrecked

Probably one of the reasons that children enjoy adventure stories is that they know everything will turn out fine in the end. In the "happily ever after" story, each disaster heightens the expectation of the reader. Everyone knows that the worse the problems get, the better the ending will be.

If you're determined to trust Jesus and live for Him, you're one of the characters in a real-life, "happily ever after" story. Not only is there heaven at the end, but your Heavenly Father has designed your life to bring glory to himself—the difficulties you face are op-

portunities for Him to work His miracles. But God won't work miracles unless you trust Him. Unbelief can make your whole life a dreadful struggle.

Paul demonstrated faith that overcomes the worst of situations. He was aboard a ship during a storm so bad that nobody except Paul expected to survive. But Paul prayed and listened to God's voice. He encouraged everyone else and assured them that God said they would live. When they landed on the island of Malta, they were well treated. Paul's faith was a testimony to everyone on the ship and he was able to preach the gospel to the whole island.

However, if he had had a complaining "this interrupts my schedule" attitude, Paul would have hated the whole winter he spent there. Have you learned how to trust God and enjoy being shipwrecked?

"But soon a tempestuous wind, called the northeaster, struck down from the land; and when the ship was caught and could not face the wind, we gave way to it and were driven. And when neither sun nor stars appeared for many a day, and no small tempest lay on us, all hope of our being saved was at last abandoned. As they had been long without food, Paul then came forward among them and said, 'Men, you should have listened to me, and should not have set

sail from Crete and incurred this injury and loss. I now bid you take heart; for there will be no loss of life among you, but only of the ship. For this very night there stood by me an angel of the God to whom I belong and whom I worship, and he said, "Do not be afraid, Paul; you must stand before Caesar; and lo, God has granted you all those who sail with you." So take heart, men, for I have faith in God that it will be exactly as I have been told. But we shall have to run on some island'" (Acts 27:14, 15, 20-25).

1. What had God told Paul?
2. Paul was so certain of their survival that he told everybody else the next morning. Because he believed God, how was Paul able to help others?
3. Do you see any way that your lack of faith in God is hindering you from helping others?

Either the Mountain or the Faith Will Have to Go

When you decide to trust God completely and follow the path He has for you, do you ever feel as if not just one mountain, but the entire Himalayan Range is stopping you? Moving mountains is a God-sized task. He only requires that you obey and trust Him. Don't get out your little pickax and start hacking away at the mountain yourself. Keep following God and going forward because the mountains you see up ahead aren't stopping you yet.

The mountains in your life can be removed little by little or in one chunk. They can be removed tomorrow or ten years from now. That is for God to decide. It is your job to trust God in every situation and not to depend on your feelings.

Most of us have seen Christians victoriously face terrible situations such as a death in the family, an alcoholic parent, or a crippling accident. We've also seen Christians go to pieces over minor things like a shopping trip, striking out in the ninth inning, or a sick dog! If you don't have faith in God and His Word, there will be impassable mountains at every turn. But, if you have complete confidence in God, the mountains will disappear. Either the mountain or the faith will have to go.

"And Jesus answered them, 'Have faith in God. Truly, I say to you, whoever says to this mountain, "Be taken up and cast into the sea," and does not doubt in his heart, but believes that what he says will come to pass, it will be done for him. Therefore I tell you, whatever you ask in prayer, believe that you receive it, and it will be yours' " (Mark 11:22-24).

"O my God, in thee I trust, let me not be put to shame; let not my enemies exult over me" (Ps. 25:2).

"Thou hatest those who pay regard to vain idols; but I trust in the Lord" (Ps. 31:6).

"When I am afraid, I put my trust in thee" (Ps. 56:3).

"Let me hear in the morning of thy steadfast love, for in thee I put my trust. Teach me the way I should go, for to thee I lift up my soul" (Ps. 143:8).

1. The writer of these Psalms constantly reminds himself that he is making the decision to trust God. During what situations does the writer of Psalms say, "I trust in God"?
2. Apply this to your life by listing the things for which you must trust God this week and this month. For example, write, "When I take the history test, I will trust in God" or "When I get left out by my friends, I will trust God."

Red Sea, Here I Come!

Someone has said, "God has designed each day so that we can't get through it without faith."

The twenty-four-hour period will pass whether or not we trust God and we may even still be alive at the end of it! The point is: How do we want to get through each day? The "Things are so bad they can't get any worse" and "I'll make it somehow" philosophies aren't God's ideas for how to get through a day.

Moses had a pretty tough day ahead of him. In front of him and the thousands of frightened and complaining people he was leading was the Red Sea, and behind them was Pharaoh's army. They could have voted on whether to drown or to let the army use them for target practice, hoping the arrows might run out. Instead, Moses prayed and put his faith in God. It became the most exciting and wonderful day of their lives. Walking through the Red Sea on dry ground must have been a lot of fun!

God had put the Red Sea in front of the Israelites so they would have to trust Him and so they could see His power demonstrated. He also gives *us* obstacles so *our* faith has a chance to grow. The final biology test, your first job interview, and the opening night of the school play are all opportunities for you to trust God. Then there are the bigger faith builders, like trusting God to change your father's attitude, to help you lose weight, or to show you how to overcome your shyness.

Approach the "Red Sea" in your life with faith and confidence. God put it there to strengthen your walk with Him.

"And Moses said to the people, 'Fear not, stand firm, and see the salvation of the Lord, which he will work for you today; for the Egyptians whom you see today, you shall never see again. The Lord will fight for you, and you have only to be still.' The Lord said to Moses, 'Why do you cry to me? Tell the people of Israel to go forward. Lift up your rod, and stretch out your hand over the sea and divide it, that the people of Israel may go on dry ground through the sea.' Then Moses stretched out his hand over the sea; and the Lord drove the sea back by a strong east wind all night, and made the sea dry land, and the waters were divided. And the people of Israel went into the midst of the sea on dry ground, the waters being a wall to them on their right hand and on their left" (Ex. 14:13-16, 21, 22).

"By faith the people crossed the Red Sea as if on dry land; but the Egyptians, when they attempted to do the same, were drowned" (Heb. 11:29).

1. What was God's command to the people?
2. Why might the command have seemed unreasonable?
3. Are you willing to obey God, to walk into your "Red Sea" and let God do the rest? What is God asking you to do now?

Week Five

YOU CAN'T BE A DO-YOUR-OWN-THING CHRISTIAN

God Doesn't Owe You an Explanation

Do you boil with anger when your father says, "Don't ask me why. Just do it because I said so"? Do you think that all authorities, including God, should give explanations before issuing orders? Have you decided that you'll always give the reasons for your instructions when you're the one in authority?

Wait a minute. Would a three-year-old accept your explanation of why string beans are better for him than M&M's? Can a fourth grader comprehend that high school math will require knowledge of the multiplication tables? Do you give a five-minute lecture on the dangers of going the wrong way on a one-way street when the girl driving your car puts on the left-turn signal? Or do you just scream, "Don't go down that street!"?

God made you. Your very existence depends on Him and He owes you *nothing*—not even an explanation. God has a right to act or to give you orders whether or not you understand. You are obligated to obey God even if you don't agree with Him.

Great peace comes to the person who admits that God is God, and that He has a right to demand anything He wishes. If you decide to become your own authority, selfishness and rebellion will enslave you. You may often get your own way, but that won't make you content. Relax and let God be your authority.

"Who has measured the waters in the hollow of his hand and marked off the heavens with a span, enclosed the dust of the earth in a measure and weighed the mountains in scales and the hills in a balance? Who has directed the Spirit of the Lord, or as his counselor has instructed him? Whom did he consult for his enlightenment, and who taught him the path of justice, and taught him knowledge, and showed him the way of understanding?" (Isa. 40:12-14).

1. Why does God have a right to tell you what to do?
2. Is there any reason for you to question whether God's commands are good for you?
3. Which of God's commands have you been questioning?

Freedom and Railroad Tracks

A train locomotive decided that it was tired of running back and forth on the same boring track. The unhappy train thought of the adventure and excitement it was missing because it had to run on tracks. However, jumping the tracks resulted in a horrible crash. Too late, the train realized that even if there had been no crash, it was impossible to go anywhere without tracks. The locomotive in the story needed a "heart transplant"—some great change within it to make it enjoy running on the track, and to be thankful for the track.

Do regulations seem confining to you? Do you hate being told what to do? Can you find fifty exceptions to every rule you're given? Jesus can change you from the inside so that you want to obey God's rules.

Just remember that God gave us rules so that we could be happy, so that we'd stay on the track and not ruin our lives.

Freedom without limits is not freedom. The freedom of speech guaranteed in the Constitution is not the freedom to yell "fire" in a huge auditorium just to prove to your friend that it does take more than five minutes to evacuate the building. It is not freedom for you to test the maximum volume of your band's new loudspeaker system at 2:00 a.m.

You don't allow a two-year-old to play with a butcher knife or eat five chocolate bars in a row, even if the kid thinks you are strict and mean. We are God's two-year-olds who don't know what is best for us. We're also trains which God made and He knows the track we are to run on.

"And all these blessings shall come upon you and overtake you, if you obey the voice of the Lord your God" (Deut. 28:2).

"You shall not take the name of the Lord your God in vain; for the Lord will not hold him guiltless who takes his name in vain. . . . Honor your father and your mother, that your days may be long in the land which the Lord your God gives you. You shall not kill. You shall not commit adultery. You shall not steal. You shall not bear false witness against your neighbor. You shall not covet [desire for yourself] your neighbor's house; you shall not covet your neighbor's wife, or his manservant, or his maidservant, or his ox, or his ass [donkey] or anything that is your neighbor's" (Ex. 20:7, 12-17).

1. Do you really believe that obeying God—regardless of how difficult it seems now—is the way to a happier and more fulfilling life? If you don't, ask God for the faith to believe that.
2. Carefully study each of the commandments given on the previous page and write down all the different kinds of trouble you would avoid if you obeyed each one of them.

But I Want My Own Way

Nothing can cause you to *want* to obey your teachers, your principal, your boss, and your parents unless two issues are settled in your life.

First, you must be willing to *obey God regardless of what He asks you to do.* Then you will be willing to obey His delegated authorities as well. Your parents may have been wrong for grounding you when car trouble, miles away from a phone, was the only reason for your coming in at 3:30 a.m. Yet, if you love Jesus so much that honoring your parents is more important to you than being wrongly accused, you'll willingly stay grounded.

Second, you must *have faith in the God who changes people and situations.* If God did not have supernatural power, then obedience to delegated authority would not seem reasonable. But God can use your obedient spirit and your prayers for your boss, teachers, and parents to *change* them. If your English teacher is constantly crabby and your father seems unreasonable, determine to obey them, to make life easier for them, and to pray every day that God will transform their lives.

There may come a time when you will have to go against authority in order to obey God. Your English teacher may assign a book that you as a Christian have no business reading. First talk with the teacher and volunteer to read another book, even if it is a longer one. If this does not work, respectfully explain your position to your teacher and be willing to take a lower grade. But as you pray for that teacher, expect God to change her attitude. Remember that God runs this universe, and He will take full responsibility for His obedient children.

"Nebuchadnezzar said, 'Blessed be the God of Shadrach, Meshach, and Abednego, who has sent his angel and delivered his servants, who trusted in him, and set at nought the king's command, and yielded up their bodies rather than worship any god except their own God' " (Dan. 3:28).

"Bid slaves to be submissive to their masters and to give satisfaction in every respect; they are not to be refractory [stubborn], *nor to pilfer* [steal], *but to show entire and true fidelity* [faithfulness], *so that in everything they may adorn* [add beauty to] *the doctrine of God our Savior"* (Titus 2:9, 10).

1. In light of the verses from Titus, does it seem possible to obey God if you are disobeying those in authority over you?
2. Are you willing to obey God in all things and to trust Him with the consequences?
3. Who is the person you are most afraid to obey? Pray for a submissive attitude toward that person and ask God to change him or her.

Obedience Made Simple

The greatest freedom in the world is the freedom to do God's will and enjoy it. This freedom can be yours because a "heart transplant" occurred inside you when you invited Jesus into your life.

The Spirit of Jesus within you loves to obey God's laws, but you keep the Holy Spirit in a cage, locked up so that His wishes are not fulfilled in your life. Instead of getting your direction from the Holy Spirit within you, you take your cues from the people around you.

A popular football player says, "Miss Strawmat is a mean teacher. She must have been a member of the Gestapo." You immediately squelch the conscience inside you that says, "Don't complain." Instead you chime in, "She has a thousand and one rules. She should teach in Siberia next year. The Communists would love her."

When the "lights out" rule is given at camp, you listen to the girl who says, "We never get to have any fun," and disregard the voice of the Holy Spirit which tells you to respect those in authority. Then your next comment is something like, "Well, we could sneak out."

We are to listen to the Holy Spirit's voice inside us and obey Him. He will gently tell us what is the next little step of obedience we need to take. That's different from listing one hundred and ten rules, trying to obey them in our own strength, and becoming nervous wrecks by thinking of do's and don't's all the time. Obeying the Holy Spirit is simple. If the Bible says, "Children obey your parents," obey them.

"For this is the love of God, that we keep his commandments.

And his commandments are not burdensome" (1 John 5:3).

"Be subject for the Lord's sake to every human institution, whether it be to the emperor as supreme, or to governors as sent by him to punish those who do wrong and to praise those who do right. For it is God's will that by doing right you should put to silence the ignorance of foolish men. Live as free men, yet without using your freedom as a pretext for evil; but live as servants of God. Honor all men. Love the brotherhood. Fear God. Honor the emperor" (1 Pet. 2:13-17).

1. Why shouldn't obeying God's commandments be burdensome?
2. What are the right reasons for obeying authority? What are the wrong reasons?
3. God commands us to honor every person. Who are the people that you are not respecting as you should? First confess this lack of respect as sin. Then pray for each of those people.

Mopping Floors and Obeying God

What does obeying God have to do with scrubbing the restaurant floor every night whether or not it needs it? Does God really care if you do the three-page assignment given to the whole class because five kids threw spitballs? Does God expect you to stay after school for talking in health class when the teacher singled you out of a group of chattering students? These are very important questions and you may not like God's answer.

God insists on obedience to authority and He gave bosses, teachers, policemen, and principals their jobs and their authority. Disobeying their authority is just like disobeying God.

The Bible says: "Let every person be subject to the governing authorities. For there is no authority except from God, and those that exist have been instituted by God. Therefore, he who resists the authorities resists what God has appointed, and those who resist will incur judgment" (Rom. 13:1, 2).

This does not mean that the person in authority is always right, but it does mean that your attitude must be one of willingness to obey. You may suggest to your boss that your time would be better spent cleaning the kitchen than mopping the floor again, but you must do it with a humble spirit and a willingness to obey. You must look at such issues from the point of view of the teacher or the boss. The only time you can disobey authority is when you are asked to go against one of God's specific commands. Even then, your attitude must be one of humility.

Honestly facing the issue of obedience to authority will convince you that you need God's supernatural power. If you ask Him in faith, He will teach you how to submit to authority.

"Slaves, obey in everything those who are your earthly masters, not with eyeservice, as men-pleasers, but in singleness of heart, fearing the Lord. Whatever your task, work heartily, as serving the Lord and not men, knowing that from the Lord you will receive the inheritance as your reward; you are serving the Lord Christ" (Col. 3:22-24).

1. Why can't you use the excuse that you shouldn't have to obey an unfair teacher or a crabby boss?
2. Do you do your algebra problems to please Jesus and do you carry out groceries to please Jesus? If you do, you can cheerfully do your best even if the person in authority over you is unfair.
3. Make a list of the disagreeable things you'll be required to do this week. Pray about each of them and determine to do them for Jesus.

Super-Snots and Cracks in the Earth

What things do you fear most? Maybe you fear failure because you want to make something out of your life. Maybe you're afraid you'll never get married and live a lonely life or that you just won't be able to stay off drugs. The thing you should fear most is becoming a rebellious person.

God says, "For rebellion is as the sin of divination [witchcraft]. . ." (1 Sam. 15:23). God can do nothing for you as long as you're rebellious, and neither can anyone else.

The seeds of rebellion can be found in words, in statements like,

"Mother, I'm going out with Dick whether you like it or not," or, "That teacher is dumb and I don't have to listen to him," or, "The pastor's sermons are stupid. I'm not going to church anymore."

Actions can also display rebellion. Walking out and slamming the door in the middle of your father's lecture, purposely asking a dumb question to interrupt the geometry teacher's explanation, or doing a sloppy job of snow shoveling to pay back Mrs. Jones for the big fuss she made when you hit a baseball through her porch window last summer are ways of showing rebellion.

Many people regard rebellion, particularly among youth, as normal. Actually, rebellion is possibly the most dangerous thing in the world. It can wreck your life and lead you far from God. Watchman Nee says, "The sin of rebellion is more serious than any other sin."

The scene is a barren desert and the Israelites are on their way from Egypt to Canaan. The trip will last forty years along the wilderness route because of their sin. Korah's complaints against Moses, who was God's chosen authority over them, were a form of rebellion against God and God considered rebellion a very serious matter.

"[Moses] *said to Korah and all his company, 'In the morning the Lord will show who is his, and who is holy, and will cause . . . him whom he will choose . . . to come near him.' And Moses sent to call Dathan and Abiram the sons of Eliab; and they said, 'We will not come up. Is it a small thing that you have brought us up out of a land flowing with milk and honey, to kill us in the wilderness, that you must also make yourself a prince over us? Moreover you have not brought us into a land flowing with milk and honey, nor given us inheritance of fields and vineyards. Will you put out the eyes of these men? We will not come up.' And as he finished speaking all these words, the ground under them split asunder; and the earth opened its mouth and swallowed them up, with their households and the men that belonged to Korah and all their goods"* (Num. 16:5, 12, 13, 14, 31, 32).

1. Where do you see rebellion in your life? Confess it to God.
2. Do you fear rebellion enough to do everything possible to avoid it?

"You Mean My Logic Could Be Improved?"

You can't retain the right to reason everything out for yourself unless you reject God's authority and become your own god. The "Do-what-you-think-is-right, to-thine-own-self-be-true" philosophy is older than Socrates. If it is carried to its logical extreme, people will be torturing and killing others because they think it is the right thing to do. The foolishness of such an idea is obvious. Yet, we often fail to see how subtly that philosophy erodes our Christianity and ruins our lives.

The Bible says, "Love is not jealous," period (1 Cor. 13:4). "Logic" can answer, "But it's only normal that since Greg is my boyfriend, I don't want him to talk to other girls." Real love comes from God. It can give without receiving and it can trust God for personal relationships. True love is not jealous, no matter how often books, movies, TV shows, or kids at school tell you differently. God says that love is not jealous. Even Dear Abby would tell you that extreme jealousy will drive Greg away from you. But you still mix logic with God's truth and that gets you into trouble.

The Bible also says, "He who believes will not be in haste" (Isa. 28:16) and, "[God] works for those who wait for him" (Isa. 64:4). Yet many Christians make "I-can't-stand-this-one-more-minute" decisions and pretend they received guidance from God. People who trust God don't leave home, quit school, stop working, or decide to get married on the spur of the moment. You shouldn't even join the football team, drop out of band, or change to an easier math class without making it a matter of serious prayer.

Your logic may scream, "I must make a drastic decision NOW!" but the Lord will answer, "Be still and know that I am God" (Ps. 46:10). Either make God your authority or follow your own logic. You can't have it both ways.

"For although they knew God they did not honor him as God or give thanks to him, but they became futile in their thinking and their senseless minds were darkened. Claiming to be wise, they became fools" (Rom. 1:21, 22).

" 'But they say. . . , "We will follow our own plans, and will every one act according to the stubbornness of his evil heart" ' " (Jer. 18:12).

1. How does God describe man's logic when it contradicts God's truth?
2. Do you have any plans you are unwilling to let God change? If so, discuss them with God.
3. The Holy Spirit wants to crush your pride and "capture" every one of your thoughts. Are you willing to let the Holy Spirit use God's Word to tell you what to think?

Week Six

"AND, LORD, THANK YOU FOR MY PARENTS"

Parents—The Forgotten People

One of the easiest ways by which to disobey God is to show disrespect for your parents. God commands you to honor your father and your mother. Regardless of their faults and failures, God wants to use your parents to shape your life.

You are like a diamond in the rough and God uses those in authority over you, especially your parents, to chip away the jagged edges and help you become the kind of person you should be. Your parents are more aware of your disagreeable personality traits and bad habits than anyone else and they are in the best position to help you change them. When your mother corrects you for putting everything off until the last minute, God is reminding you that He wants you to change in that area. Unless you listen to your mother and act on her advice, you will be hindering God's plan for your development.

Your parents, whether they are Christians or not, know your strengths and weaknesses. Even parents who don't set a good example themselves often know what's best for their children and give them good advice. I knew a man dying of alcoholism who insisted that his daughter not drink at all. He didn't follow his own advice, but he knew what was best for his child.

Determine to obey God by respecting your parents and listening to their advice. Pray for your parents and love them. If you don't, there will always be unresolved problems in your life. If you disobey your parents, you disobey God and that is a very serious matter.

"The eye that mocks a father and scorns to obey a mother will be picked out by the ravens of the valley and eaten by the vultures" (Prov. 30:17).

"They were filled with all manner of wickedness, evil, covetousness, malice. Full of envy, murder, strife, deceit, malignity, they are gossips, slanderers, haters of God, insolent, haughty, boastful, inventors of evil, **disobedient to parents,** *foolish, faithless, heartless, ruthless"* (Rom. 1:29-30).

"For men will be lovers of self, lovers of money, proud, arrogant, abusive, **disobedient to (their) parents,** *ungrateful, unholy, inhuman, implacable, slanderers, profligates, fierce, haters of good, treacherous, reckless, swollen with conceit, lovers of pleasure rather than lovers of God"* (2 Tim. 3:2-4).

1. After having read Proverbs 30:17, would you say that God is only mildly interested in how you behave toward your parents?
2. Consider all the sins listed along with "disobedient to parents" in the verses from Romans and 2 Timothy. Did you realize that disobedience to parents was that bad? Discuss this with God. If He prompts you to apologize to your parents, be sure you obey.

Obedience on the Installment Plan

When your mother asks you to carry out the garbage, do you jump up and do it, or do you respond, "Okay, after this TV show is over," and mentally add, "and after I do my homework and call Sally." Then you go to bed and forget all about the garbage. I call this "Obedience on the installment plan." It's not a good idea.

Your parents have the right to ask you to work around the house. Paul, in 2 Thessalonians 3:10, commands, "If anyone will not work, let him not eat." It is unreasonable for you to expect that your parents house, feed, and clothe you without expecting you to help at home. Not only should you clean your room, wash the dishes, and mow the lawn but you should do it in such a way as to honor your parents.

If you ask your friend to help you fix the car or show you how to make buttonholes in the blouse you are making and that friend keeps putting you off, you soon get the idea that he or she doesn't want to help you. If you keep procrastinating, your parents know that you really don't want to obey them.

When your parents ask you to do something, they deserve a cheerful, "Okay, I will," followed by instant action. Jesus told His disciples, "If you love me, you will keep my commandments" (John 14:15). If you love your parents, you'll also obey them.

Perhaps you're afraid that this will cause your father and mother to take advantage of you. Or maybe you're telling yourself if you don't stick up for your "rights," no one else will. That's where faith in God comes in. Obey your parents because God commands you to do so, then let God take care of the consequences. You'll be pleasantly surprised.

" 'Let what you say be simply "Yes" or "No"; anything more than this comes from evil' " (Matt. 5:37).

" 'What do you think? A man had two sons and he went to the first and said, "Son, go and work in the vineyard today." And he answered, "I will not"; but afterward he repented and went. And he went to the second and said the same; and he answered, "I go, sir," but did not go. Which of the two did the will of his father?' They said, 'The first' " (Matt. 21:28-31).

1. What problems can you avoid by instantly doing what your parents ask you to do?
2. Why is it wrong to promise to do something and then forget to do it?
3. Is there something your parents have asked you to do that you have still not done?

"But You Don't Know My Parents!"

You may be reading all this with your heart aching, wondering how any of it can ever apply to you. You may be saying, "But both my parents are chemically dependent," or "My mom spends so much time with her new boyfriend that I never see her," or "My parents fight so much that I can hardly stand to be around the house."

The first thing you need to know is this: "Father of the fatherless and protector of widows is God in his holy habitation [home]. God gives the desolate [those who have nothing] a home to dwell in; he leads out the prisoners to prosperity; but the rebellious dwell in a parched [dry] land" (Ps. 68:5-6).

Becoming rebellious and disobedient to God and your parents will only make life more miserable for you. However, God is the "Father of the fatherless" and He will be to you all that your parents cannot be. God will give you love, acceptance, and security if you ask Him for these in faith. He wants to give you freedom from the emotional prison in which you find yourself.

Pray for your parents and ask God to give you directly all that your parents cannot give you. Find another Christian you can confide in and ask that person to pray for you and your family. God's plan is to use the problems you've had with your family to make you a more sensitive and understanding person who can help others.

"Children, obey your parents in the Lord, for this is right. 'Honor your father and mother' (this is the first commandment with a promise) 'that it may be well with you and that you may live long on the earth.' Fathers, do not provoke your children to anger, but bring them up in the discipline and instruction of the Lord" (Eph. 6:1-4).

"The king's heart is a stream of water in the hand of the Lord; he turns it wherever he will" (Prov. 21:1).

1. Notice that the passage from Ephesians does not say, "Children obey your parents if they are *good* parents." What promise is given to people who obey their parents?
2. What command does God give to parents? Your parents are re-

sponsible to God, but it is not your job to force your parents to change.
3. If God can change the heart of a king (Prov. 21:1), do you think He can change the hearts of your parents? Spend some time in prayer determining to obey your parents and asking God to change them where they need changing.

That Monster Called Anger

"My parents make me so mad. . . ." Have you ever said that? When your father bawls you out for the mess your brother made, and when your parents in a remarkable moment of agreement decide that you should stay home from the basketball game to baby-sit, do you have a right to be angry? God says you don't. I'm not talking about the anger you'd experience if you saw a ten-year-old bully beating up on a helpless three-year-old girl. That anger would drive you to protective action. I'm talking about the anger you feel *when things don't go your way.*

Why are you so irritated if supper isn't ready and you have to eat cereal instead of roast beef before you go to be the hero of the championship game? Why can't you take it in stride when your father isn't home with the car and it's time for you to go to work? If you're honest, you'll have to admit that it's because you feel you are more important than the other people in your family.

If you gave up the right to have things go your way, the anger wouldn't even be there. Try it the next time when your clumsiness exasperates your mother, you have an accident with your dad's car, or you have to admit to your parents that you forgot to mail the envelope with the rent check. Just say, "Lord, I give up the right to be angry. I will face the consequences of my actions without feeling that I'm special and should be exempt from the trials of ordinary mortals."

If you keep giving up your right to be angry, God can start a miracle in your life. It's not instantaneous, but when you honestly praise God when things go wrong and other people treat you unfairly, God will change you.

"Let all bitterness and wrath and anger and clamor and slander

72

be put away from you, with all malice, and be kind to one another, tenderhearted, forgiving one another, as God in Christ forgave you" (Eph. 4:31, 32).

"A soft answer turns away wrath, but a harsh word stirs up anger" (Prov. 15:1).

"He who is slow to anger is better than the mighty, and he who rules his spirit than he who takes a city" (Prov. 16:32).

1. Write out Ephesians 4:31-32 in your own words, looking up in the dictionary every word that you don't completely understand.
2. Make a list of family situations in which your soft answer would help the situation.
3. Have you ever thought that controlling your temper was the real way to be a Superman or a Wonder Woman?

Perfect Parents Are Found Only in Heaven

Don't expect your parents to be what they aren't. They have their own problems and they have hang-ups from their backgrounds that they have not yet overcome. If your mother is a "Nervous Nellie," don't expect her to calmly put on a party for you and fifty of your friends. If your father can't express his feelings and affections very well, don't expect him to initiate heart-to-heart talks.

Don't conclude that you can't talk to your parents and that they'll never understand until you honestly try. Ask your mother or your dad if you can discuss your problem at some time that's convenient for *them*. The pudding is burning, the phone is ringing, and your little sister is crying; of course, your mother doesn't seem interested in the fact that your best friend at school suddenly decided not to speak to you!

If you honestly can't talk to your parents, ask God to give you an older Christian friend with whom you can discuss difficulties in your life. God will answer that prayer. Your pastor, a youth worker, or some couple at church will be more than happy to talk to you.

Don't be jealous of your friends' parents or their family lives. Most families can put on a good front for company, but they have problems, too. Besides, jealousy is sin and you can't sin without serious consequences. God says, "For where jealousy and selfish ambition exist, there will be disorder and every vile practice" (James 3:16).

Thank God for the parents you have, even if they are not perfect. And don't wish that He had given you different parents.

"Now the works of the flesh are plain: fornication [immorality], *impurity, licentiousness, idolatry, sorcery, enmity, strife,* **jealousy***, anger, selfishness, dissension, party spirit, envy, drunkenness, carousing, and the like. I warn you as I warned you before, that those who do such things shall not inherit the kingdom of God"* (Gal. 5:19-21).

"And you covet [want what you do not have] *and cannot obtain; so you fight and wage war. You do not have because you do not ask. You ask and do not receive, because you ask wrongly, to spend it on your passions"* (James 4:2, 3).

1. What does God say about jealousy? Ask God to keep you from being jealous of someone else's parents.
2. In what areas would you like to see your parents change? Have you consistently prayed that God would change your parents? Try it.
3. Do you want what's best for your parents rather than desiring only the changes that would make your life easier?

"Thank You, Mom"

How many times have you said "thank you" to your parents this week? Did you thank your mom for fixing a good dinner or did you complain because you don't like cauliflower? Think about all the money your parents have spent on you so far. Have you ever thanked them for that? How many times have they given up buying something for the house so that you could have music lessons or go to camp? Have you said "thank you"? How many times has your mother washed the dishes so you could leave early to go to the game? Did you always remember to say "thank you"?

God commands us to be "always and for everything giving

thanks in the name of our Lord Jesus Christ to God the Father" (Eph. 5:20). There is no better way to start than by thanking God for your parents and by thanking them directly for all the things they do for you.

Your parents *need* your genuine gratitude. Thank your father every time he lets you use the car. Thank your mom for cleaning the house and comment on how nice it looks. Say "thank you" even when the blouse your mother bought on sale wasn't what you like— and even find some excuse to wear it. Pray that God will keep your mother from buying ten more just like it without your giving the "Mother, styles have changed" speech. Frequent use of just two words, "thank you," can go a long way toward improving the relationship between you and your parents.

" 'Offer to God a sacrifice of **thanksgiving,** and pay your vows to the Most High; and call upon me in the day of trouble; I will deliver you and you shall glorify me.'. . . He who brings thanksgiving as his sacrifice honors me; to him who orders his way aright I will show the salvation of God'!" (Ps. 50:14, 15, 23).*

1. What will God do for thankful people when they ask Him for help?
2. What is a better gift to God, your thankfulness or more money in the offering? What is a better gift to your parents, thankfulness or an expensive present?
3. What is *one* thing for which you can thank your parents today?

Good and Boring

Does being the "good girl" type or maintaining the "nice boy" image seem a little boring at times? When the kids at school brag about sneaking out or badgering their parents until they get a new bike, do you have nothing to add to the conversation? The Bible has something to say on this very topic! "And let us not grow weary in well-doing, for in due season we shall reap, if we do not lose heart. So then as we have opportunity, let us do good to all men, and especially to those who are of the household of faith" (Gal. 6:9, 10).

God wants you to be a creatively thoughtful person. He wants

75

you to be a person who does nice things for others, who shows them the love of Jesus without trying to get anything in return. It's exciting to think of ways to help others and to build them up.

The best people to practice on are your parents. Have you ever thought of taking your mother out for lunch or giving her flowers when it's not her birthday or Mother's Day? Even if it's difficult to say it, tell her that you love and appreciate her. Maybe you'll have to start by giving her some thank-you notes or special cards. One of the very best gifts you can give to her is doing your work without being reminded and doing extra jobs you're not asked to do. She'll probably faint the first time you say, "Mother, you look tired tonight. Is there anything I can do to help you?"

What your father wants most from you is respect. Listen to him. A few "when I was a boy" stories won't hurt you. In fact, if you ask some questions, you'll learn some very interesting things both about your father and life in the past. Ask your father for advice on what subjects to take at school, on what job you should apply for, and on whether or not you should buy a car. Follow his advice and let him know that he is a very important person.

Establish a good relationship with your parents based on kindness, thoughtfulness, and generosity. There is nothing you can do that will better prepare you to be a good husband, wife, roommate, or friend.

"Let love be genuine; hate what is evil, hold fast to what is good; love one another with brotherly affection; outdo one another in showing honor. Never flag in zeal, be aglow with the Spirit, serve the Lord" (Rom. 12:9-11).

"Now who is there to harm you if you are zealous for what is right?" (1 Pet. 3:13).

1. Do you look at doing right as a challenge to be enjoyed or as a boring necessity?
2. Ask God to show you specific ways to love your parents.
3. Make a list of thoughtful things your parents would appreciate and decide to do one of them each day this week.

Week Seven

GOD AND YOUR WORK

Do You Have a Goal?

Are you a straight-pin Christian—"pointed" in one direction and "headed" in the other? Would you like to be a missionary to Japan one day and a professional race driver the next? Are you planning a camping trip one minute and staying home to bathe the dog the next? Do you study hard for a month and then consider dropping out of school? Are you enthusiastic about your job the first week but ready to quit after the boss criticizes your work?

Jesus' life was not like that. He didn't flit from one thing to another. He had one goal and everything He did was related to that great goal. That goal was so important that He could say, "My food is to do the will of him who sent me, and to accomplish his work" (John 4:34).

Jesus' life had peace and order. If you are a follower of Jesus, you are to be like Him. You must first settle the main issue. Is your goal to please God and not yourself? If it is, two practical suggestions will help you.

First, *finish what you start.* If you followed this motto, you'd spend more time praying about what you should start. The Bible has many verses which tell us to wait on God and to wait for God, but not one that says, "If you don't like it and it gets hard, quit, leave or change your mind."

Second, remember that *it is NEVER God's will for you to do nothing* for a long period of time. Although the saying, "An idle mind is the devil's workshop," is very old, it is also very true. Get a job, even if it is not the job you'd choose. Stay in school even if it's hard. God did not intend your life to be an extended vacation.

"Now we command you, brethren, in the name of our Lord Jesus Christ, that you keep away from any brother who is living in idleness and not in accord with the tradition that you received from us. For you yourselves know how you ought to imitate us; we were not idle when we were with you, we did not eat any one's bread without paying, but with toil and labor we worked night and day, that we might not burden any of you." (2 Thess. 3:6-8).

1. What does God have to say about your not doing any work around the house?

2. What's wrong with the idea, "Well, I'll just take a year off and not do anything"?
3. What would you say to someone who says, "The Lord will provide for me. I just go from place to place. I don't have to waste my time working—and I can always go on welfare"?

God Doesn't Stay Home from School

Do you sometimes say, "Do I have to go to school today?" or, "Why do I have to work tonight?" Do you hate school and dislike your job? Maybe your attitudes need some reconsidering.

God has placed you in your school and at your job to be a missionary. You may be the only Christian that some of these people will ever know well. It's your job to pray for them, to be a Christian example, and to witness. In high school you'll get to meet a greater variety of people than you'll ever know again in your whole life; as an adult you'll choose your friends according to common interests and the people at your job will automatically have similar concerns and educational backgrounds. God is just as interested in how well you behave at school, how well you do your homework, and how well you do your job as He is in your church activities. Central High or your job at Burger King is *your* "Christian service." God wants to bless your school or your place of work because of you, and He has a special purpose for your being there.

The "I'm the lonely picked on Christian" complex is not necessary. Start praying and try to find another Christian at school or at work to pray with you. Pray specifically for your school or your place of work. God has great power and He can change your boss, your teachers, your peers, the whole atmosphere—and most of all, He can change you! The problems at work or school are miracle possibilities. God does go with you and He doesn't stay home from school.

"We who first hoped in Christ have been destined and appointed to live for the praise of his glory" (Eph. 1:12).
"I am your brother, Joseph, whom you sold into Egypt. And now

do not be distressed, or angry with yourselves, because you sold me here; for God sent me before you to preserve life. So it was not you who sent me here but God . . ." (Gen. 45: 4, 5, 8).

1. Why is it wrong for you to say, "I don't like school and I don't see any purpose in attending classes"?
2. What should be your attitude if your teacher or your boss dislikes you or wrongs you?
3. Do you daily pray in faith that God will change you and your impossible work or school situation?

Don't Quit Just Because It's Hard Work

Do you realize that the command, "Six days you shall labor and do *all* your work" (Ex. 20:8) is in the Ten Commandments? S. I. McMillen, a physician, writes, "We do not understand the chemistry involved, but it is a well-recognized fact that physical work is both a preventative and curative factor in a number of mental disturbances."* God commands you to work and work is good for your health!

Laziness, selfishness, and the desire to have time for ourselves often keeps us from the hard work necessary to wax the car, write a good term paper, or keep the yard looking good. A friend of mine once came home from a Christian conference declaring that God had told him to clean his room. I thought that was a strange and rather unspiritual command until I saw his room! Messiness or lack of organization can make us very ineffective and the only cure for either one is a willingness to work hard.

God not only has individual work projects that are His will for us, but also group projects such as redecorating the church, raising money to support an orphan in the Philippines, or helping an elderly lady move. Working together can be a way of worshiping God.

The story of Nehemiah is a good example of how God's will can only be accomplished by hard workers who "stick with it." The

---

*S. I. McMillen, *None of These Diseases* (Old Tappan, NJ: Revell, 1963), p. 121.

Babylonians had completely destroyed the city of Jerusalem and taken the Jews as captives to Babylon. Years later the Persians allowed the Jews to return to the ruined city, but it was not safe to live there until a wall was built. Their enemies tried to stop the work by both armed attacks and false rumors. Through obedience, faith, and an unbelievable amount of hard work, the wall was completed.

If these people had stopped building the wall because of backaches, vacation plans, and fatigue, history would have been different. A proper attitude toward work is the key to success and victory.

"So we built the wall; and all the wall was joined together to half its height. For the people had a mind to work. So the wall was finished on the twenty-fifth day of the month Elul, in fifty-two days. And when all our enemies heard of it, all the nations round about us were afraid, and fell greatly in their own esteem; for they perceived that this work had been accomplished with the help of our God" (Neh. 4:6; 6:15, 16).

"Whatever your hand finds to do, do it with your might" (Eccles. 9:10).

1. What attitude did the people in Nehemiah's time have toward work?
2. In what ways did their work bring honor to God?
3. Examine your own attitudes toward work. Ask God to show one specific change He wants you to make in your attitudes or your work.

Doing the Dishes for Jesus

Do you realize that your homework, your job performance, and your attitude toward the chores you do around the house are terribly important to Jesus? Our self-centered society has the idea that a person can quit his job any time he or she wishes regardless of how it will affect other people. Another very popular idea is that no one should have to do anything he or she does not like. When a job becomes difficult or a class requires a lot of work, the first thought is to find an easier way.

This philosophy makes sense if there is no purpose in life except to get as much pleasure out of seventy years as possible. However, that is not God's intention for our lives. We were put on earth to prepare for eternity, to bring honor to God, and to let God work through us to restore peace in our tiny corner of His universe. God through the Holy Spirit will give us all the power we need to live like that.

Our honesty, willingness to do the hard jobs, and faithfulness to our word can help bring people to Jesus. When the work is hard and we feel like quitting, we can offer it as our sacrifice to Jesus and receive His strength to do it. When we work for Jesus and feel His approval, the fact that other people don't notice or criticize won't be that important.

A Middle Ages monk named Brother Lawrence delighted in the presence of God as he daily scrubbed the pots and pans for the monastery. Do you clean your room or wash the dishes or mow the lawn for Jesus? Do you do algebra problems for Jesus or seek to honor Him in the way you make French fries or carry out groceries? You can offer your work as worship to God.

"Whatever your task, work heartily, as serving God and not men" (Col. 3:23).

"So God created man in his own image, in the image of God he created him; male and female he created them. And God blessed them, and God said to them. 'Be fruitful and multiply, and fill the earth and subdue it; and have dominion over the fish of the sea and over the birds of the air and over every living thing that moves upon the earth' " (Gen. 1:27, 28).

1. When you work, who are you actually serving?
2. "Subduing" (controlling) the earth does include things like weeding the garden, taking out the garbage, organizing your biology notebook, and washing the car. Work is God's plan for you. In what area have you been "slacking off"?

Noah—The Man Who Started BEFORE It Rained*

Procrastination is "no" on the installment plan. A group of students in the school where I taught weren't particularly happy about the principal's new list of school regulations; one stated that a student could be suspended for insubordination to a "reasonable request." They formed the "later" gang. Rather than saying "no" to teachers' requests, they'd just say, "later." Needless to say, the instructors weren't overjoyed by their delaying tactics. The boys in the group knew that saying "later" had the same result as saying "no."

---

*Title used by permission from *Serendipity*.

One of the problems with putting everything off until the last minute is that once we've waited long enough, it's literally impossible to do what we set out to do. If you've stayed in bed until 7:30, you can't get to first-hour class on time. If you've waited until the night before the semester project is due, it may be impossible to finish the assignment on time. The devil likes to fool you into thinking that you're just a last-minute person and that the world should make allowances for you.

One of the bad things about procrastinators is that they tend to be dishonest in making excuses for their inaction. But if you didn't ask anyone to be on the program until the day before, you can't say that it had to be cancelled because of lack of cooperation. If you waited until the last minute, you don't have a right to complain about the unreasonable assignment. If you started twenty minutes late in the first place, it's not honest to blame your tardiness on a two-block detour.

Imagine Noah standing in the rain, trying to come up with a good excuse for why the ark wasn't finished yet. If he had procrastinated in building that boat, you and I wouldn't be here today!

God wants to make you into a Noah who plans ahead and works hard so that His work can be accomplished through you.

"Slothfulness [laziness] *casts into a deep sleep, and an idle person will suffer hunger"* (Prov. 19:15).

"I passed by the field of a sluggard [lazy person], *by the vineyard of a man without sense; and lo, it was all overgrown with thorns; the ground was covered with nettles, and its stone wall was broken down. Then I saw and considered it; I looked and received instruction. A little sleep, a little slumber, a little folding of the hands to rest, and poverty will come upon you like a robber, and want like an armed man"* (Prov. 24:30-34).

1. What excuses do you think the man in Proverbs 24 had for not weeding his vineyard?
2. Why do you think he didn't fix the stone fence?
3. Do you have any "fences" that need mending or "vineyards" that need weeding? Which job that you've been putting off would God have you work on today?

"Can't We Have a Picnic Before We Go into the Ark?"

If you think about the people of the Bible, and other people throughout history that God has greatly used, there doesn't seem to be a procrastinator in the bunch. Noah started the ark, Abraham left for Canaan, Moses faced Pharaoh, and Joshua took Jericho— immediately. Paul did not take three years off for a Mediterranean cruise and some sun on a Greek island. Elijah didn't come late to the contest on Mount Carmel. Mary didn't argue that she was still too young to have a baby.

The issue of obeying God always comes down to what we plan to do about it *right now.* Most of us feel that if God asked us to do something "important," such as building an ark or talking to a king, we wouldn't procrastinate. It's just that we prefer to put off "unimportant" things, such as cleaning our rooms, turning in algebra assignments, and writing thank-you notes. We fail to realize that each time we put something off, we are forming a habit. Bad habits are not easily broken. Procrastination will soon turn into laziness.

God puts a very high priority on the habit of faithfulness—being completely dependable. Jesus said, "He who is faithful in a very little is faithful also in much; and he who is dishonest in a very little is dishonest also in much" (Luke 16:10). A good worker does not keep putting things off.

I once read a book by Watchman Nee entitled *The Normal Christian Worker.* I expected great and deep spiritual truths. I was a little disappointed when the entire first chapter talked about diligence. It could be summed up in this quote: "It is in fact essential to say, and to say with emphasis, that a Christian worker must be a person who has a will to work."* Just being a good worker who wouldn't procrastinate or side-step responsibility didn't seem especially great or spiritual. However, the more I've thought about it and observed Christian workers, the more I see the truth of Nee's statement. Many of us need to confess unwillingness to work hard, as a sin. Let God remake you into a hard-working Christian.

---

*Watchman Nee, *The Normal Christian Worker* (Hong Kong, Church Book Room, 1965), p. 3.

"Go to the ant, O sluggard [person who is habitually lazy or idle]; *consider her ways and be wise. Without having any chief, officer or ruler, she prepares her food in summer, and gathers her sustenance* [food] *in harvest. How long will you lie there, O sluggard? When will you arise from your sleep?"* (Prov. 6:6-8).

"He who is slack in his work is a brother to him who destroys" (Prov. 18:9).

1. What does the Bible have to say about poor work habits, laziness, and procrastination?
2. Why does God use something so tiny as an ant as an example for us?
3. Discuss your school work, your job, and your household chores with God. Do you have some attitudes God wants to change?

"But I Always Get Stuck Mopping the Floor!"

Are you sick of being the doormat? Would you like to carry an early American flag—the one with the rattlesnake and the caption, "Don't tred on me"? Do you get the worst schedules at work because you complain the least? Are you tempted to talk back the way everyone else does? Does the boss always make *you* mop the floor at clean-up time?

First you need to ask God to show you how to be happy in your present circumstances. Someone has quipped, "Bloom where you're planted. Then maybe God will move you to a bigger pot." Paul says, "I have learned, in whatever state I am, to be content" (Phil. 4:11). God will bless your decision to get all your approval from Him. Don't worry that no one will recognize your genius, appreciate all your hard work, or listen to your great ideas. Thank God for your school and for your job, just the way it is.

Step two is the frosting on the cake, but you have to bake the cake first. After you have told God you're willing to put up with anything and that you'll trust Him, start praying for changes—not a new location but improvements in your present situation. Once your bitterness and rebellion are gone, God will answer those prayers and teach you how and when to appeal to authority that is unjust.

God will show you how to defend your answer to the history teacher in a respectful and acceptable manner. He'll make someone else request to work every Saturday night or He'll cause the new Christian kid to be transferred into your biology class so that there are two of you who believe that God created the world. He'll show you how to ask for time off to go to the Christian retreat and how to enjoy mopping the floor. If your school or work situation were perfect, you'd miss out on a lot of exciting answers to prayer.

"There is great gain in godliness with contentment" (1 Tim. 6:6).

"Now to him who by the power at work within us is able to do far more abundantly than all that we ask or think, to him be glory in the church and in Christ Jesus to all generations, for ever and ever" (Eph. 3:20, 21).

1. Have you tried "godliness with contentment"?
2. Do you believe that God can do even more than you ask or think in your school or at your job?
3. What one improvement in your situation will you pray for this week?

Week Eight

THE CHRISTIAN FAMILY CIRCLE

Penetrating Pride and Prejudice

As you listen to the news, you hear of tension between races, nations, and economic groups. There is so much suspicion and lack of understanding among people of different backgrounds that peace and even common sense decisions seem impossible.

Jesus came to give you genuine love and understanding for all people. Individuals from all races, languages, and cultures belong to the body of Christ. People who love the same Lord and belong to the same body have *everything* in common.

God can use you as a living advertisement to show His love which can build bridges over the chasms of pride and prejudice. Ask Him for a close friendship that will be an example to the rest of the world. Maybe He wants you to be a helpful friend to a senior citizen and show the world that with Jesus there is no generation gap. Maybe there is a handicapped person who needs a friend with extra patience. The Lord might lead you to a person of another race or ethnic background. Maybe He wants you to befriend someone from the poorest part of town. Be willing to go beyond the comfortable clique of kids who are just like you.

In order to demonstrate the love of God, you must also love and pray for the people in your church who seem to be prejudiced or narrow-minded. Jesus loves people even when they are wrong. Prejudiced people don't need more information; only Jesus can change inner attitudes. However, their seeing the love of Jesus in another person may penetrate the walls prejudice has constructed. They just may ask Jesus to give them that kind of love.

"There is neither Jew nor Greek, there is neither slave nor free, there is neither male nor female, for you are all one in Christ Jesus" (Gal. 3:28).

"My brethren, show no partiality as you hold the faith of our Lord Jesus Christ, the Lord of glory. For if a man with gold rings and in fine clothing comes into your assembly, and a poor man in shabby clothing also comes in, and you pay attention to the one who wears the fine clothing and say, 'Have a seat here, please,' while you say to the poor man, 'Stand there,' or, 'Sit at my feet,' have you not made distinctions among yourselves, and become judges with evil thoughts?" (James 2:1-4).

1. Why is prejudice against any person or any group of people wrong?
2. What prejudices do you see in your own life?
3. Describe the kind of people you like most to be around. List a few people whose company you don't especially appreciate. Ask Jesus to help you treat all members of His body equally and to give you love for those who you would not normally choose as friends.

Attention, Lone-Ranger Christians

An eye, arm, or leg that is not attached to the body is completely useless. A body functions as a *unit*. Can you imagine a body which has one hand trying to feed the mouth while the other is trying to spill the food? An eye doesn't close its lid to sleep while the other is intently focusing on a TV show. An ear doesn't try to be a hand and a liver doesn't insist on being seen by everyone. The red corpuscles don't compete with each other to see which one can be biggest and most important. Neither is there any place for a "Do-Your-Own-Thing," Lone-Ranger Christian in the body of Christ.

You are not so holy, intelligent, and talented that no church is good enough for you. You don't have some special calling that no other Christian can understand. You are not so advanced that you don't need the advice of other Christians. God can't tolerate a "nobody's going to tell me what to do" attitude. The Bible warns against "neglecting to meet together as is the habit of some" (Heb. 10:25).

You are also to honor those in authority in the church or in the Christian group that you're a part of. If you have a spirit of pride and rebellion, you can be dead wrong, even if you are right. Anyone will be attracted to a group where there is genuine love, humility, and caring, regardless of the lousy program. On the other hand, God can't work, even if your youth presentation is good enough for television, if dissension, quarreling and bad feelings are included in the production of the show. God can use you only if you willingly learn from other Christians and are subject to the authority of your pastor and other Christian workers.

"Likewise you that are younger be subject to the elders. Clothe yourselves, all of you, with humility toward one another, for 'God opposes the proud, but gives grace to the humble' " (1 Pet. 5:5).

"Let the elders who rule well be considered worthy of double honor, especially those who labor in preaching and and teaching" (1 Tim. 5:17).

"Who is wise and understanding among you? By his good life let him show his works in the meekness of wisdom. But the wisdom from above is first pure, then peaceable, gentle, open to reason, full of mercy and good fruits, without uncertainty or insincerity" (James 3:13, 17).

1. What kinds of attitudes are you to have toward other Christians? List them.
2. Can you find attitudes in your life that are not consistent with these scriptural guidelines? Talk this over with God.

3. Elders are pastors or Christian leaders. What is to be your attitude toward them? (Notice that the verse implies that even the elders who do not rule well are to be given honor. We are to respect the authorities God has appointed even when we do not agree with them.)

Every Body Needs a Head

Medical science has made great strides, but no one is yet proposing head transplants! The body without the head is useless since most of our movements and body functions are controlled by the brain.

The Bible says, "Christ is the head of the church, his body, and is himself its Savior" (Eph. 5:23). This means that Jesus is the authority of the church and that we are to receive our directions from Him. If we really did that, things would be a lot different.

Jesus didn't say one thing about whether the church should have modern or traditional music, but He did pray, "I do not pray for these only, but also for those who believe in me through their word, that they may all be one; even as thou, Father, art in me, and I in thee, that they also may be in us, so that the world may believe that thou hast sent me" (John 17:20, 21).

Jesus didn't tell us His views on bowling on Sunday or dress codes for church, but He did say, "This is my commandment, that you love one another as I have loved you" (John 15:12).

Jesus didn't mention what time church should start in the summer or give His opinion on whether or not youth groups should sponsor all-night parties, but He did state, "By this all men will know that you are my disciples, if you have love for one another" (John 13:35).

Before you re-enact Custer's last stand as you insist that your youth group spend the car wash money on a ski weekend, remember what happened to Custer. And more importantly, recognize that following Jesus' command to love other Christians is more significant than getting the "right" things done or expressing your opinion. It would be better to throw the money in the garbage in an attitude of love and unity than to give it to missions and end up with a quarreling, bitter youth group. Your heart attitude of obedience to

Jesus is more important than anything else because He is the head of the church.

"Rather, speaking the truth in love, we are to grow up in every way into him who is the head, into Christ, from whom the whole body, joined and knit together by every joint with which it is supplied, when each part is working properly, makes bodily growth and upbuilds itself in love" (Eph. 4:15, 16).

"If possible, so far as depends upon you, live peaceably with all" (Rom. 12:18).

1. What attitudes are you to have toward other Christians? (You are to display these attitudes even if you are right and the leaders or the majority are wrong.)
2. How does the body of Christ "upbuild itself"?
3. Ask God to show you any wrong attitudes you have toward other Christians and be willing to clear those up.
4. Can you expect to *always* be on good terms with everyone? What is your responsibility?

When Christians Are a Pain

Have you ever felt or said, "Christ is great, it's just Christians I can't stand"? Christians come in all kinds of categories. There are the easy-going, freedom-train types who seem to come along for the ride while others do all the work and take all the responsibility. There are the super-strict "I don't do all those things so I am the holiest" variety. And there are even a few older saints whose motto is, "During the American Revolution when we were growing up, Christian young people didn't go bowling and do other sinful things."

Christians come from many different backgrounds and may have bad manners, bad breath, bad grammar, or bad taste. Worse yet, Christians can sin against people. There are Christians who judge without knowing the facts, Christians who exclude others from their group because the others are different, and Christians who are too busy with their own lives to help when someone is in deep trouble.

Before you become bitter against any Christian or group of Christians, keep this in mind: It is a great offense to a parent if someone rejects his child, even if the kid is a brat. Jesus loved all His children so much He died for them. Thoughtlessness or sinful behavior on the part of a Christian hurts Jesus more than it hurts him. If Jesus can love and accept that self-centered girl, that boisterous boy, that gossiping woman, or that sarcastic man, who are we to say that we are too good to associate with such people?

The Bible clearly says that we must forgive others in order to receive God's forgiveness. If you are a Christian, you must forgive regardless of what the other person has done to you. No matter how much you have to forgive other Christians, it won't be as much as Jesus has forgiven you and He's the sinless Son of God.

Remember that you are not exactly perfect yourself. Ask God what part of the misunderstandings that you have with other Christians is your own fault. Try making a list of all the things other Christians would have to forgive you for. God can give you love for other Christians no matter who they are or what they have done.

"Above all hold unfailing your love for one another, since love covers a multitude of sins" (1 Pet. 4:8).

"Brethren, if a man is overtaken in any trespass, you who are spiritual should restore him in a spirit of gentleness. Look to yourself, lest you too be tempted. Bear one another's burdens, and so fulfil the law of Christ" (Gal. 6:1, 2).

1. In the light of these verses, what would you say to the person who says, "He's a Christian and I have a right to expect better from him"?
2. What attitudes are we to have toward other Christians?
3. Have you been excusing a bad attitude toward another Christian because the other person sinned against you? If so, discuss it with God.

So What If You're a Kidney?

"She's so talented it's sickening!"

"I wish I could play the piano the way he does."

"If I could meet people as easily as Tim does, I'd witness all the time."

Have you ever said or thought things like these? Feelings of jealousy or inferiority which often plague Christians would melt away if all of us really understood the meaning of "the body of Christ." God tells us in the Bible that all true Christians are part of His body. He is the head, and just as impulses from the brain direct the actions in our human bodies, so Jesus is to direct the actions of Christians.

You are very important and God made you with exactly the right kind of personality and abilities to best fit into Christ's body. No one can fill the place you have as well as you can. Thank God for that and ask Him how you can best be used in each situation.

In a body it would seem that the teeth, eyes, nose, and hair which are constantly seen and often admired would be the most important. But the truth is that we could live without any of those things, but we could not survive without some of the *unseen* members of our bodies such as the kidneys and the lungs.

It's foolish to be jealous of someone else's ability to speak, or play the piano, and thus hurt the whole body of Christ by not recognizing or praying about how to use your own gift for encouraging people. The people who hold churches together are not the leaders. They are people who are completely dedicated to Jesus and are quietly and obediently carrying out their functions in the body regardless of what others are doing.

Nothing will do more to make you a defeated Christian than comparing yourself with others. Follow Jesus. Do the work for Him that only you can do, and relax. You don't have to be a carbon-copy Christian and you can be free from the pressure of trying not to be a kidney.

"Peter turned and saw following them the disciple whom Jesus loved [John]. . . . When Peter saw him, he said to Jesus, 'Lord, what about this man?' Jesus said to him, 'If it is my will that he remain until I come, what is that to you? Follow me!' " (John 21:19-22).

"But as it is, God arranged the organs in the body, each one of them, as he chose. If all were a single organ, where would the body

be? As it is, there are many parts, yet one body. The eye cannot say to the hand, 'I have no need of you,' nor again the head to the feet, 'I have no need of you' " (1 Cor. 12:18-21).

1. Why shouldn't Peter have spent his time worrying about what John would do?
2. What concerns you most, your relationship with God or the spiritual report cards of the Christians around you?
3. Are you content with your place in the body of Christ and determined to be the best "kidney" or "liver" you can be?

Body Building

If one part of the body does not function properly, the other parts of the body try to compensate for the loss. For example, if the eyes cannot see, the sense of hearing becomes more keen. If one lung collapses, the whole body makes adjustments so that the other lung can supply the body with oxygen. This is the way the body of Christ should function.

If Susie forgets to bring the songbooks, you could suggest that everyone sing familiar songs rather than comment that scatter-brains like Susie shouldn't be elected youth group secretaries in the first place. If the cook on the youth retreat serves burned grilled cheese sandwiches, you could make some cheerful statement about the chile being good. Instead of criticizing the pastor for announcing choir practice on the wrong night, you could do everything possible to let people know that the night has been changed.

There is no place for criticism or putting people down in the body of Christ. We should, instead, try to cover the faults and mistakes of other Christians and pray that God will change them where they need changing. We often expect too much of other Christians and don't make the same allowances for them that we make for ourselves. Sometimes, too, we look to other Christians as examples rather than looking to Jesus. Other Christians, even leaders and pastors, are bound to disappoint us at times. We must also learn to love and pray for Christians of other churches, even if we don't always agree with them.

If you are looking at Jesus and not at other believers, the Christian you respected may fall, but that won't ruin your faith. When another Christian or group of Christians fails or sins, it's your job to help, not to criticize.

"I entreat [beg] *Euodia and I entreat Syntyche to agree in the Lord. And I ask you also, true yokefellow* [fellow worker], *help these women, for they have labored side by side with me in the gospel. . ."* (Phil. 4:2, 3).

"So if there is any encouragement in Christ, any incentive of love, any participation in the Spirit, any affection and sympathy, complete my joy by being of the same mind, having the same love, being in full accord and of one mind. Do nothing from selfishness or conceit, but in humility count others better than yourselves. Let each of you look not only to his interests but also to the interests of others" (Phil. 2:1-4).

1. What should be your attitude toward other Christians when they sin or mess things up?
2. List all the commands in the above verses that should govern our relationships with other Christians.
3. Are you willing to help two Christians who are having trouble getting along?

Caring and Sharing

It's amazing how your whole body can feel completely miserable because of a stubbed toe or a toothache. It's impossible to completely ignore a cut finger or a sprained ankle. The Apostle Paul commented, "If one member suffers, all suffer together" (1 Cor. 12:26).

You know that busyness, self-centeredness, and lack of concern have often kept you from giving help to other Christians. Your Christian friend may want someone to talk with the night you planned to study for the government test. You may have to skip bowling to make a hospital visit. Paying your friend's way to the youth retreat may be a real financial sacrifice. Yet, helping others will be exciting and will build up your own Christian life.

Let God use you to send a card of encouragement, to make a phone call to see how your friend is doing, or to talk to that older lady at church and ask her if she is feeling better. You can organize a farewell party for the shy guy who is moving with his parents to Arizona. You can faithfully write to the new Christian with the tough home situation whom you met at camp. As you give of yourself, you will grow as a Christian, experience the joy of sharing, and make an important contribution to the body of Christ.

When the cast comes off your leg, your body is relieved and when your new glasses help you see better, you feel happy inside. The body of Christ should be like that. "If one member is honored," Paul wrote, "all rejoice together." Be genuinely happy for the joys and successes of others—even when things are not going well for you. The success of one Christian is the success of all.

"Contribute to the needs of the saints, practice hospitality. Rejoice with those who rejoice, weep with those who weep" (Rom. 12:13, 15).

"Practice hospitality ungrudgingly to one another. As each has received a gift, employ it for one another, as good stewards of God's varied grace" (1 Pet. 4:9, 10.).

"But God has so composed the body, giving the greater honor to the inferior part, that there may be no discord in the body, but that the members may have the same care for one another. If one member suffers, all suffer together; if one member is honored, all rejoice together" (2 Cor. 12:24-26).

1. Which is easier for you, sharing the joys or the sorrows of other people?
2. What gifts has God given you that you can use to help other Christians? Ask God to show you what these gifts are and how you can best use them.
3. Can you think of one thing you can do to care for another Christian this week?

99

Week Nine

STANDING UP FOR JESUS WHEN THE WHOLE WORLD IS SITTING DOWN

You Start by Tearing Down the Altar

Does your heart pound violently when you think, *This would be a good opportunity to start telling my friends about Jesus*? Do you turn five shades of purple when the hockey captain mentions that you're a "holy roller" who can't even skate? Then you need to know about Gideon.

If you're a Christian who is paralyzed by fear, the devil has you just where he wants you. He'll condemn you for your fear. He'll tell you that you're a hopeless, helpless, and useless Christian who can never do anything right. He'll tell you that other Christians are different and that they don't have the same problems that you do.

How can you change from a "secret-service Christian" into a confident and courageous Christian? By obeying, not by becoming instantly fearless. Your knees may knock so much that you'd make a good addition to the percussion section of a music group, but if you obey God, He'll bless you. I've never met a Christian whom God is really using who hasn't had to go out on a limb to obey God in spite of being very much afraid.

Gideon was a real "scaredy cat." When an angel first appeared to him, he was hiding from the enemy. The first assignment God gave him was to tear down the altar of the idol Baal. Gideon did this at night because he was afraid. When God asked him to lead the army of Israel, his fear made him ask God for a special sign. He wanted to be certain God would help him. However, Gideon *always obeyed* in spite of his fear, and God gave him a great victory.

You have a choice. Will you obey God or will you give in to your fear?

"That night the Lord said to him, 'Take your father's bull, the second bull seven years old, and pull down the altar of Baal which your father has, and cut down the Asherah [female idol] that is beside it; and build an altar to the Lord your God on the top of the stronghold here, with stones laid in due order; then take the second bull, and offer it as a burnt offering with the wood of the Asherah which you shall cut down.' So Gideon took ten men of his servants and did as the Lord had told him; but because he was too afraid of his family and the men of the town to do it by day, he did it by

night" (Judg. 6:25-27). (For the whole story of Gideon, read Judges, chapters 6 and 7.)

1. What excuse could Gideon have given for not obeying?
2. Notice that God didn't start by asking Gideon to recruit an army. Neither will God have you start with your own TV show. Start by obeying when He asks you to invite your classmate to attend church with you, even if you are afraid.
3. God did not scold Gideon for being afraid and doing the job at night. God honored his obedience. Are you willing to obey even when you are afraid?

Are You a Secret-Service Christian?

Do you squirm when someone at school talks about those "stupid religious fanatics"? "Are you scared to death to witness to your new friend? Would you be willing to tell the captain of the football team or your boss at work that you're a Christian? Are you willing to stick up for Jesus any place and any time?

The first thing that you must deal with is the fear of other people. Sorting the matter out isn't difficult. Either you care about what other people think or you care about what God thinks. You can straddle the fence for a while, but sooner or later situations will arise in which you must make a clear choice between God and your reputation.

Be willing to follow God in *every* situation. If you fail, confess it, and ask God for a second chance to witness or to make a Christian stand. God is the God of the second chance. He will teach you if you're willing to let people think you are different, pathetic, or crazy.

Sometimes the fear of standing up as a Christian comes from unwillingness to live the consistent Christian life expected of a person who shares his or her faith. If your teacher knows you are a Christian, she'll expect you to do your homework. If your teammates know you are a Christian, they'll watch how you react when you fumble twice in one game. Bosses think Christians should be

good workers. Are you willing to constantly live your Christianity and risk ridicule?

There is a legitimate fear of making a fool of yourself. Fear of doing something that would tarnish God's reputation. You don't have to put Bible verses on your letter jacket, preach hellfire and brimstone sermons in speech class, and carry a ten-ton Bible to prove that you're a Christian. Ask God to free you from fear of what other people will think, and to give you His wisdom and discernment in all you say and do.

"For I am not ashamed of the gospel: it is the power of God for salvation to every one who has faith, to the Jew first and also to the Greek" (Rom. 1:16).

"Are not two sparrows sold for a penny? And not one of them will fall to the ground without your Father's will. But even the hairs of your head are numbered. Fear not, therefore; you are of more value than many sparrows. So every one who acknowledges me before men, I also will acknowledge before my Father who is in heaven; but whoever denies me before men, I also will deny before my Father who is in heaven" (Matt. 10:29-32).

1. Why shouldn't we be afraid to witness?
2. If you're not ashamed of Jesus, what promise can you claim?
3. Think of the people who especially frighten you. Pray for them and ask God for the courage to be a Christian testimony to these people.

A Plane with Two Wings

"If you live a good enough life, you don't have to say anything. People will just come up to you and ask you what makes you so different."

Have you ever heard that? Well, it isn't in the Bible. The Bible commands us to *preach* the gospel (which takes some speaking). New Testament Christians were always witnessing verbally.

Words are not enough, though, because what you *say* you believe will mean nothing unless your *life* measures up.

Someone once asked, "What is more important in my Christian witness, the words I say or the kind of life I live?"

The answer given was, "Which wing of an airplane is most important, the right one or the left?" Obviously, we need both!

In this day and age when people are into all kinds of bizarre religious cults, being "different" is hardly noteworthy. In fact, most people would consider it impolite to ask why you are different. Although non-Christians may see in a believer a quality of life that's beautiful and unique, few would feel comfortable asking about it. Yet, many people long to have someone ask them personally if they have accepted Jesus Christ and know they are going to heaven.

In the Bible we read, "He who winneth souls is wise" (Prov. 11:30, KJV). Trust Jesus to show you how to be an effective Christian witness. There will be awkward moments and uneasiness when you face new situations; but the joy of realizing that you may meet some person in heaven because God used your witness is worth it all. The thrill of doing the most important task in the universe, and having Jesus give you the needed on-the-job training is much greater than the thrill of making the football team or receiving a full-tuition scholarship to the college of your choice.

"And how are they to believe in him of whom they have never

heard? And how are they to hear without a preacher?" (Rom. 10:14).

"We have renounced [given up] disgraceful, underhanded ways; we refuse to practice cunning or to tamper with God's word, but by the open statement of the truth we would commend ourselves to every man's conscience in the sight of God. And even if our gospel is veiled, it is veiled only to those who are perishing. In their case the god of this world has blinded the minds of the unbelievers, to keep them from seeing the light of the gospel of the glory of Christ, who is the likeness of God. For what we preach is not ourselves, but Jesus Christ as Lord, with ourselves as your servants for Jesus' sake" (2 Cor. 4:2-5).

1. What reasons do you find in these verses for witnessing *verbally*?
2. How does the devil (the god of this world) try to keep people from accepting Jesus?
3. How can we be sure that we are really preaching Jesus and not ourselves?

Let the Holy Spirit Be Your Coach

You may be wondering, *How can a shy and timid person like myself ever witness to anybody? How can I keep from sounding like a little robot who spouts off the same words to everyone without being sensitive to their needs? How will I know when to keep quiet and when to speak? How will I know what to say?*

Someone has said, "The answer to every 'how question' in the Christian life is the Holy Spirit." The Holy Spirit can make a naturally shy person into a bold witness. The Holy Spirit can tell you the right words to say at the right time and can show you when to keep silent.

You experience the power of the Holy Spirit by spending time in prayer, by being willing to obey instantly, and by having faith that the Holy Spirit will act. It has been said, "If you're not spending more time talking to God about people than talking to people about God, something is wrong." Pray for the people you'd like to witness to, and pray for them every day.

When you know you should say something, say it. Get the first

106

word out and the Holy Spirit will bless your obedience by giving you the right things to say.

There are other things you can do, too. Take a class on evangelism techniques so you can learn better how to share your faith. Lend or give away good Christian books. Invite people to church and Christian club meetings. Some letters you write will give you a good opportunity to share Christ. Always remember that your obedience to God, not necessarily the response of the people to whom you witness, is the important thing. Ask God to give you opportunities to witness and He will answer that prayer.

"Not by might, nor by power, but by my Spirit, says the Lord of hosts" (Zech. 4:6).

"Behold, I send you out as sheep in the midst of wolves; so be wise as serpents and innocent as doves. Beware of men, for they will deliver you up to councils and flog [whip] you in their synagogues [churches], and you will be dragged before governors and kings for my sake, to bear testimony before them and the Gentiles. When they deliver you up, do not be anxious how you are to speak or what you are to say; for what you are to say will be given to you in that hour; for it is not you who speak, but the Spirit of your Father speaking through you" (Matt. 10:16-19).

1. What things can you depend on the Holy Spirit for in witnessing?
2. Do you really trust the Holy Spirit, or do you try to witness in your own strength?

Are You Working for Jesus or for Audience Applause?

"But I can't teach a Sunday school class or speak in front of a group, or go witnessing door-to-door, or . . ."

Well, if you can't you may just be the right person for the job. God isn't looking for the smooth, super-talented, showy worker who will expect the attention and applause of every onlooker. God is after the person who will serve Him in deep humility and will acknowledge his complete dependence on God at all times.

This doesn't mean God wants choirs made up of monotones, a blind man to drive the church bus, and a guy who wears eighteenth-century clothes to start a Bible study in your high school. It also doesn't mean that God doesn't care whether or not you practice your solo or prepare your lesson. It does mean that no effective spiritual work can be accomplished without complete dependence on God, and without a sense that you're working for Him because you love Him.

If you're really dependent on God, whether you succeed or fail will be *God's* concern, not yours. As an employee in a restaurant it is your responsibility to do your job well. You let the owner worry about whether or not the restaurant is making a profit. Even so, God's big requirement from you is faithfulness. The Holy Spirit will take the responsibility for success or failure. God requires diligence, regardless of the response or the obstacles.

The Bible promises that in "due season" we'll reap (harvest) if we don't give up. And God decides when "due season" is, not us! As soon as we become totally involved in the number of people we witness to, the number of hours we spend preparing, the number of people who come to our special Christian club social, or the number of compliments the quartet receives, we're not thinking of Jesus at all.

We like to do the jobs at which we excel and the ones we feel comfortable doing. Jesus, our Boss, may decide that a position in which we feel very uncomfortable will best build our character. It brings great glory to God when someone demonstrates God's power by letting God accomplish through him or her what would naturally be impossible. Let Jesus decide what you should do and how you should do it.

"Moreover it is required of stewards [people entrusted with responsibility] *that they be found faithful"* (1 Cor. 4:2, KJV).

"But we have this treasure in earthen vessels [clay pots] *to show that the transcendent* [extraordinary] *power belongs to God and not to us"* (2 Cor. 4:7).

1. Remember that you're only the clay pot and that the power is the Holy Spirit within you. How will that change your attitude toward your ability to do Christian work?

2. In what area does God want you to be faithful right now? Are you obeying Him?
3. Are you willing to let God decide whether you are a success or a failure?

"Pardon Me, Your Attitude Is Showing"

We live in a world where people admire how many A's one gets on his report card, how many home runs one hits, or how much money one makes each week. Most people could care less if the person worked for the A's so his father would buy him a car, bribed the pitcher of the opposing team, or got his good job because his boss owed his father money. Everything seems to be measured by output and performance, not by motives and heart attitudes. Working for Jesus is the exact opposite. In God's book *obedience* is the important thing.

If you're proud because you're the only person your age who goes door-to-door witnessing with your church every Sunday, you're not really obeying God. He hates pride. If you're inviting people to church just to win a prize at the end of the month, your motives are wrong. If you think you know the best way to win your school to Christ and go against the authority of your youth advisor, God cannot bless your work; the Bible says, "You that are younger be subject to the elders." If you and another Christian quarrel over the best way to share your faith, neither of you is walking very close to Jesus. If you just rattle off a spiel to a person so you can say you witnessed, without loving and caring for the person, it's wrong. Scripture tells us we are to be "speaking the truth in love."

Your witnessing will have no lasting effect if it is done with the wrong motives. That does *not* mean that you are excused from sharing your faith. Jesus commands us to "go into all the world and preach the gospel" (Mark 16:15). James 4:17 also tells us, "Whoever knows what is right to do and fails to do it, for him it is sin."

"And you became imitators of us and of the Lord, for you received the word in much affliction, with joy inspired by the Holy

Spirit; so that you became an example to all the believers in Mace-
donia and in Achaia [provinces of Greece]. *For not only has the*
word of the Lord sounded forth from you in Macedonia and Achaia,
but your faith in God has gone forth everywhere, so that we need not
say anything" (1 Thess. 1:6-9).

1. Why didn't Paul have to say anything to the Thessalonians
   about their responsibility to witness?
2. Do you know a Christian whom you could imitate?
3. Evaluate your actions and motives. Would you want someone to
   imitate your Christian life?

Christians and Opinion Polls

The devil is very sneaky. He is always trying to make you feel
like Dumbo the Defeated Christian. Your brother sneers, "I thought
Christians were supposed to be generous, but when I borrow money,
you want it back right away. I'm surprised you don't charge inter-
est."

Then your teammate says, "Well, for a guy who prays about
playing baseball, you sure do strike out a lot."

Your boss may not be able to resist saying, "If you weren't a
churchoholic, it would be a lot easier to make up the schedule
around here."

You can allow people's expectations to put you into a pressure
cooker or else you can live to please God. The Lord requires a lot
from you, but He has also given you the supernatural power of the
Holy Spirit to live the Christian life. Always pray about the critical
comments of non-Christians, especially those who are always trying
to trap you. If God convicts you of wrongdoing, confess it and determine to change. If the statement has no basis, ignore it. You are living to please God, not to get a better rating in the opinion polls.

Constantly remember that the power to be a good Christian witness must come from God and not from you. Throughout the day
talk to God. Pray, "Lord, you know I hate getting bad grades on
tests. I give my chemistry grade to you. I also trust you for the test
I'm going to get back today," or, "God, you know what the locker
room is like. Show me exactly what to say if I get teased again to-

day," or, "Lord, give me the courage to write my English theme on 'Jesus, my best friend.' "

Live only to please Jesus. Let Him take care of the reaction of others. When you trust the Holy Spirit for power, the Christian life becomes one of victory.

"Therefore since we are surrounded by so great a cloud of witnesses, let us also lay aside every weight, and sin which clings so closely, and let us run with perseverance [patience] *the race that is set before us, looking to Jesus the pioneer and perfecter of our faith, who for the joy that was set before him endured the cross, despising the shame, and is seated at the right hand of the throne of God. Consider him who endured from sinners such hostility against himself, so that you may not grow weary or fainthearted"* (Heb. 12:1-3).

"If you are reproached [criticized] *for the name of Christ, you are blessed, because the spirit of glory and of God rests upon you"* (1 Pet. 4:14).

1. Even though lots of people are watching you, who should you be looking at?
2. How can Jesus' example help you?
3. If you trust God, how will He reward you when other people make fun of you for being a Christian?

Week Ten

EVERYDAY EVANGELISM

Hostages in the Dungeon of Despair

One ordinary Saturday morning Jewell called. She was my co-worker in Christian youth work. She sounded discouraged. The club president was unreliable, hardly anyone was attending, and the Bible study groups were faltering. I listened for a while to the facts which I already knew.

I finally said, "Hold on. I remember reading a verse this morning in 2 Timothy 4: 'Preach the word, be urgent in season and out of season.' I guess it must be the 'out of season' time right now. Encouragement from God's Word came to our rescue. Neither of us has ever forgotten that morning.

If you try to reach the world for Jesus, the devil will be there with missiles: B-52 bombers, tanks, and even BB guns from his arsenal marked, "Discouragement." If you are planning to rely on your own enthusiasm, he will shoot you down. If you're not obeying Jesus out of love and not getting your power from the Holy Spirit, Christian work will be a real drag.

The real reason we should witness is because Jesus told us to, not because people need us. For example, the inhabitants of Asia certainly needed Jesus, but Paul was "forbidden by the Holy Spirit to speak the word in Asia." Paul and his friends finally went to Macedonia.

If we're witnessing just to help people, it's all too easy to be overly concerned with their responses. We will become discouraged when things go wrong or people don't like what we say.

Jesus' love should keep us from discouragement. The person who really loves us will eat our burned toast with a smile or appreciate the fact that we stopped to buy flowers even if the shop had none left. Jesus totally loves us, and He is very pleased with our sincere obedience regardless of how others respond to our witness.

We must look to the Holy Spirit for the power, the joy, and the love that we need. His supply is limitless, so there is no need for discouragement. If we descend into "the pits," it's only because we have cut off our supply of love, power, joy, and peace by looking only at ourselves or at the work we are doing.

"So we do not lose heart. Though our outer nature is wasting

away, our inner nature is being renewed every day. For this slight momentary affliction is preparing for us an eternal weight of glory beyond all comparison, because we look not to the things that are seen but to the things that are unseen; for the things that are seen are transient [temporary], *but the things that are unseen are eternal"* (2 Cor. 4:16-18).

1. How can our inner nature be "renewed every day"?
2. Do you keep your focus on Jesus or on your accomplishments?
3. Are you willing to work for Jesus even if it's "out of season"?
4. What circumstances are you looking at now instead of looking at Jesus? Pray about those things now.

Truth and Worshipers of the Great Pumpkin

Have you ever wondered why outwardly sincere, nice people can believe garbage? Why does the girl who used to attend your Christian group become a Moonie, a Great Pumpkin worshiper, or a member of the Divine Light Mission? Some people with high I.Q.'s think that God is dead, that a certain diet makes one spiritual, or that the stars tell the future. It's heartbreaking when the kid who was seemingly excited about Jesus all of a sudden decides he's an atheist, that living with his girlfriend is okay, or that Zen-Buddhism is the real answer. Why do these things happen?

Sin in a person's life opens the door for the devil's deception. The devil is always trying to fool people into believing things that are not true. But the person who is completely willing to give up sin and to seek Jesus will find Truth. Jeremiah 29:13 states, "You will seek me and find me; when you seek me with all your heart."

Actions change because of an accompanying change in belief. For example, that guy who decided to move in with his girlfriend will usually have doubts about the Bible being the word of God. Otherwise it's uncomfortable to be found directly disobeying God.

Deciding that there is no God gives a person unlimited freedom. Trying to find a church that will approve of one's behavior is another way out. Others have secret yearnings to display intellectual

115

knowledge and to win arguments. Many cults provide them with this opportunity.

One lesson a missionary must learn is that God has given people free wills. A person can *choose* to follow Jesus or to disobey God. If a person does not accept Christ, it doesn't necessarily mean that there is something wrong with the missionary or the way the message is presented.

"The coming of the lawless one by the activity of Satan will be with all power and with pretended signs and wonders, and with all wicked deception for those who are to perish, because they refused to love the truth and so be saved. Therefore God sends upon them a strong delusion, to make them believe what is false, so that all may be condemned who did not believe the truth but had pleasure in unrighteousness" (2 Thess. 2:9-12).

1. What things does Satan do to try to deceive people?
2. Why are people fooled by Satan's lies?
3. Do you always love God's truth? What are the consequences of rejecting it?

Pearls, Pigs, and Perishing

Deception (believing what is not true), comes from unwillingness to accept God's truth. Therefore, you must beware of people involved in cults and false teachings. Their power comes from Satan and he is very dangerous. Pray for the deceived person who is about to become one of the guru's assistants. Warn him or her if the warning will be heeded. However, if the person wants to argue, don't keep talking. God will give special grace and protection in handling such people with whom you must associate, but in witnessing situations be careful of those who want to destroy Christians.

Jesus himself cautioned us, "Do not give dogs what is holy; and do not throw your pearls before swine [pigs], lest they trample them under foot and turn to attack you" (Matt. 7:6). There are deceived, godless people who will turn and attack you. Don't be guilty of the pride which says, "I'm so strong in my beliefs that nothing anyone could do or say will hurt me." That's not true. Satan is working through many people and he is very strong. Let God guide you and don't foolishly and wrecklessly decide that with your great Bible knowledge you can convert the cult leader. Obey Jesus' warning. Use great caution and much prayer.

Stay away from religious arguments. You will never argue anyone into the Kingdom of God. If you're a good debater, you may enjoy the challenge, but this isn't doing God's work. If your discussion is unreasonable, if neither of you is listening to and trying to understand the other person's viewpoint, change the subject and don't cast your pearls before swine.

"But avoid stupid controversies, genealogies [lists of people's ancestors], *dissensions, and quarrels over the law, for they are unprofitable and futile. As for a man who is factious* [fond of stirring up arguments], *after admonishing* [warning, cautioning, advising] *him once or twice, have nothing more to do with him, knowing that such a person is perverted and sinful; he is self-condemned"* (Titus 3:9-11).

"Alexander the coppersmith did me great harm; the Lord will requite [pay back] *him for his deeds. Beware of him yourself, for he strongly opposed our message"* (2 Tim. 4:14, 15).

1. What's wrong with the statement, "Never give up on witnessing to a person no matter what, because that's showing love"?
2. According to Titus 3:9-11, what's the scriptural method of handling a person who loves to argue and to destroy the unity of true Christians?
3. Sometimes pride makes us want to convert the toughest candidate first. Alexander was just such a candidate. What advice did Paul give to Timothy, a very strong Christian? Why?

"The World's Falling Apart— Maybe I'd Better Save It"

You don't want to be a Christian who lives as though football scores and new clothes are the most important things in life. Yet, the "doomsday is just around the corner; don't buy any extra frozen pizza because Jesus may come tonight" people make you feel uncomfortable. Just how are you supposed to react to the fact that the world is falling apart and desperately needs Jesus? The most important thing you can do to evangelize the world is to pray for other people.

Jesus spent much time teaching His disciples to pray, but the gospels don't mention His giving any preaching lessons. Jesus told His disciples, "The fields are white unto harvest," meaning that there were a lot of people out there just waiting to accept Jesus. But He didn't organize a witnessing marathon to see who could win the most converts. Instead He told them to "pray therefore the Lord of the harvest to send out laborers into his harvest." Praying for people is the most important work in evangelism.

Thousands of people in India die every day without Christ. When you hear that don't leave your parents and take the next plane to Bombay. But don't wring your hands in despair either. Decide that you'll pray that God will send missionaries to India. Obviously, someday you could be part of the answer to your own prayer.

Don't give up when your friend suddenly becomes a vegetarian, an atheist, and a homosexual. Even if that friend won't listen to a word you say, there is hope. Your prayers, not your brilliant statements, will bring your friend to Jesus.

People who learn to pray will make the greatest contribution to this falling-apart world.

"And he said to them, 'The harvest is plentiful, but the laborers are few; pray therefore the Lord of the harvest to send out laborers into his harvest' " (Luke 10:2).

"First, I thank my God through Jesus Christ for all of you, because your faith is proclaimed in all the world. For God is my witness, whom I serve with my spirit in the gospel of his Son, that without ceasing I mention you always in my prayers" (Rom. 1:8, 9).

1. How was Paul helping the people in Rome whom he had never seen? (He did want to go to Rome to preach, but he knew that only his prayers would pave the way for that.)
2. Ask God to help you pick out a mission "field"—some country of the world to which you can be a missionary right now through your prayers.

Welcome to the World's Greatest Enterprise

Do you ever dream of being the jungle pilot who brings the missionary doctor the right medicine just in time to save the village? Of being a great evangelist speaking in front of thousands of people? Of being the heroine who liberates with the gospel the women of the Muslim world? Dreams are great and reaching the world for Jesus is the most exciting project to give your life to. It's the world's greatest enterprise. However, there are some pitfalls to avoid.

The devil loves dreamers who contemplate great and glorious plans but *do* practically nothing. If you have lofty hopes of becoming a foreign missionary (and even if you don't), it is more important right now that you be a missionary and a witness where you are. There is nothing magical about being a staff member of a Christian organization, speaking Spanish, or taking a trip across the ocean. Being a missionary is being committed to the project Jesus started when He came to earth, that of telling the good news to every person.

The only way that any part of your dreams will come true is if you start *right now.* Take a friend out for a Coke for the specific purpose of telling him or her about Jesus. Give a speech on "What Jesus Means to Me" in speech class. Visit a neighbor in the hospital and give him a good Christian book to read. Get permission from neighborhood parents and start a Bible club for their little kids.

Don't become a "the grass is always greener someplace else" dreamer. God has different ministries for different churches and Christian organizations. Find the place God has for you and stay there. Serve faithfully, even if others are retreating or looking for a spot where they would have a better chance to become heroes. It's not the realization of *your* dream but the fulfillment of *God's* plan for you that makes you a success in the world's greatest enterprise.

"He first found his brother Simon, and said to him, 'We have found the Messiah' (which means Christ). He brought him to Jesus. Philip found Nathanael, and said to him, 'We have found him of whom Moses in the law and also the prophets wrote, Jesus of Nazareth. . .' (John 1:41, 42a, 45).

"So the woman . . . went away into the city, and said to the peo-

ple, 'Come, see a man [Jesus] who told me all that I ever did. Can this be the Christ?' They went out of the city and were coming to him. Many Samaritans from that city believed in him because of the woman's testimony. . ." (John 4:28-30, 39).

1. All of us should study our Bibles and learn all we can so we can better communicate our faith. But do we have to know a lot before we start witnessing? Why or why not? (The above verses will help you.)
2. How were history and heaven changed by the witness of the people mentioned in the above verses?
3. What do the Scripture passages teach you about witnessing?

Jungle Tribes, Headhunters, Roast Monkey and YOU

When you think of "mission field," all kinds of exotic pictures probably fill your head: grass huts, witch doctors, lepers, and Buddhist temples, to mention a few. They seem unreal and far away. Yet, as a Christian, you should be concerned that all people everywhere hear about Jesus. The Bible talks much about missions. The book of Acts is filled with missionary adventures. Jesus even left heaven to be a "foreign missionary" to planet earth.

Jesus' final orders teach us that the purpose of Christians on earth is to reach the world for Christ. The Holy Spirit was given to convict people of sin and to draw them to Jesus. The Holy Spirit is the number one missionary in the world.

Everyone wants to be part of a great cause, an earth-shaking revolution which will affect the world for eternity. Christian missions is that cause. There have been great changes for the better in places where the gospel was preached and part of the population became Christians. Biographies of great pioneer missionaries like David Livingstone, Hudson Taylor, and William Carey are exciting and inspiring. Even more exciting is the fact that you can be part of this great enterprise which was started by Peter, Paul, and the other apostles, and will not end until Jesus returns.

Get to know a missionary personally and pray for the work he is

doing. Write letters, without expecting answers, to encourage that missionary. Ask for the name of a teenager in a foreign country that you can specifically pray for. Give money for missions, even if you have very little. You and your friends, your Sunday school class, or your Christian club can support a foreign orphan. Be willing to *go* as a missionary if that is God's plan for you.

" 'Go therefore and make disciples of all nations, baptizing them in the name of the Father and of the Son and of the Holy Spirit, teaching them to observe all that I have commanded you; and lo, I am with you always to the close of the age" (Matt. 28:19, 20).

"But you shall receive power when the Holy Spirit has come upon you; and you shall be my witnesses in Jerusalem and in all Judea and Samaria and to the ends of the earth" (Acts 1:8).

"And every day in the temple and at home they did not cease teaching and preaching Jesus as the Christ" (Acts 5:42).

1. How do we know that we are responsible for telling others about Jesus?
2. Ask Jesus to show you one thing you can do this week to help spread the gospel.

Picking Priorities

One of the devil's chief tactics is making people so busy with *good* things that they have no time for *God's* priorities: Bible study, prayer, witnessing, helping lonely people, and encouraging other Christians. Your life is most likely too busy already. If you look around at the Christian adults you know, you can see how easy it is to be so occupied with "living" that Christian things have to be sandwiched in here and there.

Is Jesus your *number-one* priority? You may be able to say "yes" and mean it, but practical everyday decisions will decide whether or not you'll spend a lot of time with Jesus. Many couples have gotten so engrossed in planning a wedding, building a house, or getting ahead in their careers that they have nearly forgotten one another. And it wasn't because they didn't love each other.

If spending time with Jesus and doing the things He considers most important are to be first in your life, you must rearrange your whole schedule. Your personal relationship with God will come first. For example, you won't skip devotions and church to study for the biology test. You'll put Jesus first and let Him take care of everything else. Doing what He wants will be top priority with you. Perhaps you'll miss a day of skiing with your friends in order to do something that will mean a lot to your mother. You'll cancel a date (if you're dating the right kind of person that person will understand) to spend extra time with the friend whose father just died.

Working for Jesus may mean getting by on less money and working fewer hours, being willing to drop out of a sport for a while, or giving up your three favorite TV programs. It's more important to make weekly calls to the kids who should be attending your youth group and to find more time for Bible study.

Telling other people about Jesus is greater than getting straight A's, making money so you can have a car, or having the right clothes, the perfect haircut, or an even tan. Let Jesus decide what your priorities should be.

"But seek first his kingdom and his righteousness, and all things shall be yours as well" (Matt. 6:33).
"For whoever would save his life will lose it; and whoever loses his life for my sake, he will save it" (Luke 9:24).

1. What things do you like to do best? Are you willing to give up these things so that you will have more time for God's work *if* Jesus asks you to do so? (God wants us to live *balanced* lives. Our willingness to give up everything for Him often frees us to be more efficient people who accomplish God's work and have time left over for our own special interests.)
2. Ask Jesus for the faith to believe that He means what He says about giving us everything we need if we put Him first.

Week Eleven

HELPLESS BUT NOT HOPELESS—
STRENGTH TO LIVE THE JESUS LIFE

Trying to Hold On by the Skin of Your Teeth

We were playing volleyball at a Christian camp. One of the guys had just received Jesus as his Savior and was going home to a tough situation. He lamented, "I wonder how long I can hold out as a Christian once I get home."

That fellow didn't really know or trust the Holy Spirit. He was trying to live the Christian life in his own strength. To survive physically you must breathe in air constantly. Similarly, the Holy Spirit maintains His work constantly in the life of a person who is born again of the Holy Spirit of God. We can put our faith in the Holy Spirit. An oak tree or a St. Bernard becomes large because of the spirit of life inside. Likewise, the Holy Spirit inside us will mold us and make us grow more like Jesus *if we let Him work.* Through our own efforts we can't even hold on by the skin of our teeth.

The Holy Spirit within us is the constant source of power to live the Christian life. The Holy Spirit was the power that raised Jesus from the dead, and that power lives in us! This becomes real in everyday life if we exercise faith that the Holy Spirit is in us. We demonstrate this faith by keeping our hands off and letting the Holy Spirit work.

It's like inviting a world famous chef to cook a dinner in your kitchen for your friends. If you really trust him, you won't constantly remind him that dishes are breakable, ask him to leave out the onions, and keep turning the steak so that it won't burn. You won't even worry about dinner being late. You will only ask if there is anything you can do to help.

Just as the chef would produce a delicious dinner, the Holy Spirit will create in you Christian growth and maturity if you let Him work in any way He chooses in your life.

"For God is at work in you, both to will and to work for his good pleasure" (Phil. 2:13).

"May you be strengthened with all power, according to his glorious might, for all endurance and patience with joy" (Col. 1:11).

"And [Jesus] said, 'The kingdom of God is as if a man should scatter seed upon the ground, and should sleep and rise night and day, and the seed should sprout and grow, he knows not how. The

earth produces of itself, first the blade, then the ear, then the full grain in the ear. But when the grain is ripe, at once he puts in the sickle, because the harvest has come' " (Mark. 4:26-29).

1. Why would you think it crazy for a farmer to spend sleepless nights worrying about whether or not his crops will come up?
2. What advice would you give to the farmer who studied day and night and was completely frustrated because he couldn't *understand* how his crops grew?
3. Are you willing to simply trust the Holy Spirit to work in your life, even if you don't see daily visible results?

Act Like a Branch

Once upon a time there was a little branch near the bottom of a large, beautiful apple tree. This little branch named Twigger was most unhappy. He envied the branches that were bigger than himself and those on the top of the tree which had a better view than he. He hated wind storms, winter snows, and kids climbing on him. He didn't like the way he was shaped and considered himself rather ugly. He tried unsuccessfully to have the most blossoms.

Twigger eventually discovered that all these thoughts of jealousy, worthlessness, dissatisfaction, self-centeredness, and competition filled him with a poison. The poison counteracted the power of the sap which came from the trunk. When spring came, there was not a blossom on him! When fall came, he had no apples to show for his work!

Twigger became so worried he even prayed, "Please make me a branch. Please make me a branch that will bear fruit."

The branch next to him overheard his prayer and said, "That's a silly prayer. You *are* a branch and the trunk has plenty of sap for you. If you'd stop making it impossible for yourself to receive the sap, things would change."

Twigger thought, *I may be brown and fruitless but I am a branch. The trunk has the life-giving power I need. I must stop resisting this power and stop trying to run my own life and being dissatisfied with my position.*

Twigger soon realized the vast amount of power that the trunk

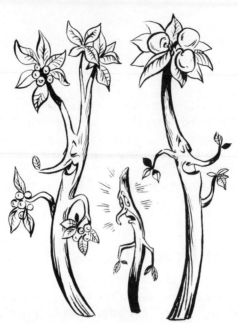

had. It was right that the trunk give him orders and that he be completely dependent on the trunk. All of a sudden, he was thankful to be a branch—just a little branch on the lowest part of the tree. He was thankful for harsh weather that made the whole tree grow stronger. He was thankful for the other branches too.

And do you know what? As Twigger concentrated on the trunk, stopped blocking the sap, and started believing in the power the trunk would give, he didn't have to try to bear fruit or blossoms. *It just happened!*

"I [Jesus] am the vine, you are the branches. He who abides in me, and I in him, he it is that bears much fruit, for apart from me you can do nothing. If a man does not abide in me, he is cast forth as a branch and withers; and the branches are gathered, thrown into the fire and burned. If you abide in me, and my words abide in you, ask whatever you will, and it shall be done for you. By this my Father is glorified, that you bear much fruit, and so prove to be my disciples" (John 15:5-8).

1. Would it be possible for a branch properly connected to a healthy vine to bear no fruit?
2. Is a branch conscious of the fruit it produces? Why or why not?

3. Ask God to show you any way in which you are blocking Him from producing "fruit" in your life.

Giving Yourself to God

Have you given yourself to God? Throughout history people have done some crazy things to try to impress God. You don't have to torture yourself to get rid of all your evil desires; Jesus "bore our sins in his body on the tree, that we might die to sin and live to righteousness" (1 Pet. 2:24).

You don't have to give up your possessions and live in poverty to gain the self-discipline necessary to follow Jesus; already "God is at work in you, both to will and to work for his good pleasure."

God has already provided the power. It's our job to present ourselves to God. We become holy, not by thinking about how sinful we are, but by setting ourselves apart for God.

Have you specifically given your entire body and your possessions to God? Are your feet God's feet and therefore unable to take you to the wrong hangouts? Are they willing, no matter how tired, to take you to help a person in need? Is your tongue God's tongue so that it won't repeat gossip? Will it instead tell someone about Jesus even if you're scared to death? Is your time God's time which can't be wasted and isn't reserved only for you?

Do you think of the ten-dollar bill in your billfold as belonging to God? Are you willing to give up the new beach towel you "need" if you feel God wants you to give that money to a Christian cause?

You could become a missionary or a minister, but if you hadn't given every part of yourself to God, you wouldn't really be His. How about giving God each part of your body and each thing you own?

"Do not yield your members [parts of your body] to sin as instruments of wickedness, but yield yourselves to God as men who have been brought from death to life, and your members to God as instruments of righteousness" (Rom. 6:13).

"Submit yourselves therefore to God. Resist the devil and he will flee from you" (James 4:7).

"Do not be overcome by evil but overcome evil with good" (Rom. 12:21).

1. List all the commands of the three verses on page 129 in your own words.
2. Apply the verses with practical suggestions to the following situations: (a) Deciding not to use drugs anymore. (Example: I will remember that my body belongs to God and will make these positive steps: I will find Christian friends who don't use drugs. I will find good things to do with my time, such as getting involved in church activities and helping others. I will learn to pray about my problems. I will guard my health and do everything I can to keep my body healthy.) (b) Determining not to talk back to my parents. (c) Being willing to befriend the most unpopular kid at school. (d) Improving my poor study habits.
3. How can you resist the devil? If you resist the devil, what promise do you have?

God Has the Grace If You Have the Faith

The world is filled with unfinished projects, broken diets, and uncompleted schemes. At first it seems simple or fun to do something new and different. But it's easy for all of us to fall back into old habits.

In our Christian lives, we face the same temptation. When it finally dawns on us that we can receive salvation by faith, we decide to accept Jesus. We are overjoyed by the new discovery that we can live by faith. After a while, though, it's easy to slip back into our old patterns of seeing everything from an earthly point of view. We try to cope with things through our own efforts.

You are fortunate if you understand that your greatest danger is that of falling back into old habits of trying to live up to God's standards in your own strength. We sometimes call this "living under the law."

The problem is not God's sensible and necessary rules, or the project we started, or the healthy diet. It's just that we feel "under it" and are powerless to do what we should. Instead of living "under law," God wants us to live "under grace" (the favor and strength God gives to us as a gift). I simply have to receive what is given. God wants us to live "under grace" and have absolute faith in Him, to receive from Him all the grace and power we need to live the Christian life.

As we progress in faith, God gives us harder and harder tasks so that our faith will grow. Every situation we face and every command in the Bible is an opportunity to exercise our faith and receive God's grace. God puts our need for faith in the strongest possible terms: "For whatever does not proceed from faith is sin" (Rom. 14:23). You need the faith that asks for and expects to receive God's grace. This faith is not an optional extra for daily Christian living; it's an essential.

"Behold, he whose soul is not upright in him shall fail, but the righteous shall live by his faith" (Hab. 2:4).

"When the servant of the man of God rose early in the morning and went out, behold, an army with horses and chariots was round about the city. And the servant said, 'Alas, my master! What shall we do?' He said, 'Fear not, for those who are with us are more than those who are with them.' Then Elisha prayed, and said, 'O Lord, I pray thee, open his eyes that he may see.' So the Lord opened the eyes of the young man, and he saw; and behold, the mountain was full of horses and chariots of fire round about Elisha" (2 Kings 6:15-17). This is an exciting story. Read the entire account in your Bible!

1. Are you an Elisha or are you an "Alas, what shall we do?" person?
2. Why do you think that Elisha lived by faith and his servant didn't?
3. What "impossible" situations are you facing now? Ask God to show you the "invisible chariots of fire" around you. God has the grace if you have the faith.

New Tricks for a Teenage Dog

"But I just can't change." How many times have you heard this said? How many times have *you* said it? "You can't teach an old dog new tricks" is cited as gospel truth; it would seem heresy to imply that people and dogs were not created equal.

Saying that you cannot be different implies that the God who slung the milky way into space and invented the exact formula for water couldn't possibly do one thing with you, His creation. This is ridiculous.

God has all power and He can change you as He has changed thousands of people throughout history. John, who was noted for his quick temper, became the apostle of love. Saul, who persecuted Christians, became Paul who constantly risked his life for Christ. Scaredy-cat Peter became fearless. What made these people change? The power of the Holy Spirit.

"All of this sounds great," you may be saying to yourself, "but it doesn't work. I just can't stop being late, or sarcastic, or depressed."

The first step is to *believe* Jesus when He says, "All power is given unto me in heaven and in earth" (Matt. 28:18, KJV). Believe that includes power over *you*.

Then determine to *obey*. If you keep on obeying, leaving the supper table without dessert so that your friend won't be inconvenienced, apologizing for the sarcasm as soon as you notice it, and stopping the self-pity the minute you recognize it, sooner or later it will be automatic.

There are two types of people who attempt to quit bad habits. One triumphantly announces, "See, I tried it and I told you I couldn't stop." This type of person even implies that God is mean if He expects people not to be sarcastic. The other type of person stops every time he or she detects the least bit of sarcasm and keeps relying on God. His attitude is, "God is right and I'm wrong and I'll keep obeying Him even if I have to stop smoking 146 times."

In the Christian life there is no room for the "I am the way I am and you can't teach an old dog new tricks" routine.

"And in the synagogues immediately [Paul] *proclaimed Jesus, saying, 'He is the Son of God.' And all who heard him were amazed, and said, 'Is not this the man who made havoc in Jerusalem of those who called on this name?' "* (Acts 9:20, 21).

"After a little while the bystanders came up and said to Peter, 'Certainly you are also one of [Jesus' followers], for your accent betrays you.' Then he began to invoke a curse on himself and to swear, 'I do not know the man.' And immediately the cock crowed, And Peter remembered the saying of Jesus, 'Before the cock crows, you will deny me three times.' And he went out and wept bitterly" (Matt. 26:73-75).

"Now when they saw the boldness of Peter and John and perceived that they were uneducated, common men, they wondered; and they recognized that they had been with Jesus" (Acts 4:13).

1. What changed Peter and Paul?
2. Do you have habits or ideas that you are unwilling to let God change?
3. Ask God to show you one change He would like to make in you and cooperate with Him so He can make that change in you.

Maybe You Need a Broken Leg!

A little lamb was always running away from the flock. He rebelled against the shepherd's rules, and wrecklessly headed for trouble. Although the lamb felt he loved the shepherd and was proud to belong to him, he had big ideas to explore the world, find better pasture, and make new friends. He had his own ideas of what he wanted to accomplish.

One day the shepherd, because he loved the lamb, broke its leg. This required the lamb to stay close to the shepherd. In fact the lamb often had to be carried. The lamb developed a dependence on the shepherd. Even when the leg was completely healed, he stayed close to the shepherd and didn't wander away.

We're often like that lamb. Even things we have supposedly given to God can run wild and not be under His total control.

You may give your good singing voice to God with the idea of becoming a great Christian singer. God may have to shatter your dream of ever singing for Him until you learn to depend on Him. Many things we do for God with the best of intentions fail because God has to teach us to depend on Him. Otherwise we'll stray.

The important thing is not what you do but whether your attitude while doing it is one of total dependence on God. Jesus is the One who judges whether or not you are dependent on Him. Don't use "success" as the way of telling whether you've given yourself to Jesus. Don't depend on the feelings you have.

Don't be discouraged if all your plans for the youth retreat flop. God loves you so much that He wants you to learn absolute dependence on Him. The failure you experience when you try hard to do something for God may be His way of teaching you this all-important lesson.

Don't fall into discouragement. Fall into the arms of Jesus. As you learn to depend on Him, He can start using the things you give to Him—in ways more wonderful than you could ever have dreamed.

" 'Come, let us return to the Lord; for he has torn, that he may heal us; he has stricken, and he will bind us up' " (Hosea 6:1).

"So they sat down in groups, by hundreds and by fifties. And taking the five loaves and the two fish he looked up to heaven, and blessed, and broke the loaves, and gave them to the disciples to set before the people; and he divided the two fish among them all. And they all ate and were satisfied" (Mark 6:40-42).

1. Why do you think Jesus multipled a little boy's lunch rather than cause steak dinners to appear out of thin air?
2. What does Jesus' breaking the loaves *before* blessing them symbolize? (Watchman Nee writes, "He breaks what He takes, but after breaking it, He blesses it and uses it to meet the needs of others.")
3. What in your life needs to be "broken" before it can be blessed?

Forty Years at Desert Academy

Moses had the right intentions. Moses' fellow-Hebrews really needed help, and he was willing to help them, even at the risk of losing the throne. But Moses' helpfulness ended in disaster because he was using his own intelligence and brawn. The Bible implies that he was very smart and that he was physically very strong.

God sent Moses into a desert for forty years. There He could break Moses from the habit of depending upon himself. Then God could use him for more than Moses had ever imagined—not just to help his people *in* their slavery but to lead them *out* of bondage.

Your brilliant plans to work for God are useless. God wants you dependent on Him and His plans. Cockiness and foolhardiness are often associated with youth. However, you can skip the pitfalls of those attitudes. Come humbly before God each day and ask Him about His plans for you for that day.

Learn from the life of Moses. Humbly submit all your ideas and actions to the God of all wisdom. Develop a healthy fear of depending on yourself. Then maybe you'll "graduate" before your forty years are up.

"One day, when Moses had grown up, he went out to his people and looked on their burdens; and he saw an Egyptian beating a Hebrew, one of his people. He looked this way and that, and seeing no one he killed the Egyptian and hid him in the sand. When he went out the next day, behold, two Hebrews were struggling together; and he said to the man who did the wrong, 'Why do you strike your fellow?' He answered, 'Who made you a prince and a judge over us? Do you mean to kill me as you killed the Egyptian?' Then Moses was afraid, and thought, 'Surely the thing is known.' When Pharaoh heard of it, he sought to kill Moses. But Moses fled from Pharaoh and stayed in the land of Midian; and he sat down by a well. Now the priest of Midian had seven daughters; and they came and drew water, and filled the troughs to water their father's flock. The shepherds came and drove them away; but Moses stood up and helped them and watered their flock" (Ex. 2:11-17).

1. What was wrong with the way Moses tried to prevent his fellow Israelites from getting beaten up?
2. When Moses ran away to Midian, he found another way to be helpful. (Of course, any man would come to the rescue of seven beautiful, helpless, single women.) What did he do for them?
3. Do you have some projects, plans, or ideas for being helpful that you need to give to God? Let Him show you what to do and how to do it.

Week Twelve

HOW TO OVERCOME EVIL

Is the Devil After You?

Frazzled and Frightened finally decided to break up with her boyfriend, Super-Creep, whose selfishness knew no bounds. However, he was determined not to let her go. Therefore, she lived in constant fear of his coming to capture her.

A kindly king named Love and Mercy asked Frazzled and Frightened to marry him. He was a perfect gentleman who would love and protect her as well as supply her every need. His palace guards were strong and capable. The palace itself was a gorgeous place. The only catch was that Frazzled and Frightened would have to give up the right to make any decisions on her own. The king would take all the responsibility and would run her life.

Whether or not Frazzled and Frightened should accept the offer would depend on the king's true character. If the king were sensible, caring, and unselfish, it would be a very good arrangement.

Jesus who is all-powerful, all-wise, and all-loving makes the same offer to you. He wants to guard you from sin, keep you from wrong decisions, and protect you from false ideas. But just as I can't keep your watch safe while you swim unless you give it to me, Jesus can't keep anything of yours that you're refusing to give to Him.

What you entrust to Jesus, He is able to keep. Trust Him with your heart and your emotions. You can't keep your temper, but He can. You can't control your tongue, but Jesus can.

Maybe sometimes you feel as if the devil is after you in the same way that Mr. Creep was after Frazzled and Frightened. When the world seems like it is too much, when the news is increasingly dreadful, and when the older people initiate conversations about the younger generation going to the dogs, remember that Jesus is your keeper. He will guard you if you continually give yourself to Him. You will be safe in His care, even if atomic bombs explode and your friends forsake you.

"He will not let your foot be moved, he who keeps you will not slumber. Behold, he who keeps Israel will neither slumber nor sleep. The Lord is your keeper; the Lord is your shade on your right hand. The sun shall not smite [destroy] you by day, nor the moon by night. The Lord will keep you from all evil; he will keep your life. The Lord will keep your going out and your coming in from this time forth and for evermore" (Ps. 121:3-8).

1. What promises does God give you in this Psalm?
2. God will not guard your going out and your coming in if you've decided to go some place without Him. Is there a lack of surrender or a lack of faith that keeps one of these promises from becoming real in your life?

Look, It's an Angel, It's a Lion, It's a Serpent—It's the Devil!

The devil's only power is that of deception—making us believe his lies. Colossians 2:13-15 teaches us this: "And you, who were dead in trespasses [sins] . . . God made alive together with him, having forgiven us all our trespasses, having canceled the bond [evidence that we have sinned and broken God's laws] which stood against us with its legal demands; this he set aside, nailing it to the cross. He disarmed the principalities and powers [the devil and his kingdom] and made a public example of them, triumphing over them in him."

God has completely forgiven us. The debt of our sin has been wiped out. Yet the devil will try to make us believe that God doesn't want to forgive us or that we need to earn our forgiveness. The truth is that our sin has been nailed to Jesus' cross. It's already been taken care of. Don't let the devil deceive you with his lies.

Jesus has disarmed Satan and all his demons. He has publicly disgraced them by rising from the dead. The devil is now a defeated enemy, but he has a lot of lies.

The power of deception is very great. A robber doesn't need a loaded gun in order to force a bank teller to hand over the money. He only has to *convince* the teller that the gun is loaded.

If a beautiful girl can be convinced that she's ugly, such deception will affect her whole life.

The devil is a master con artist. Never feel that you have figured out the devil's strategies and can counter them. You can't. Jesus is the only one strong enough to defeat Satan. Resist the tendency to "take it easy" and to stray from Jesus "just a little." The devil will exploit that kind of attitude. Any pride or untruthfulness on your part is a hole in your defenses that the devil will be certain to notice. You will be safe only when you carefully follow and obey Jesus.

"And no wonder, for even Satan disguises himself as an angel of light" (2 Cor. 11:14).

"Be sober, be watchful. Your adversary [enemy] *the devil prowls around like a roaring lion, seeking some one to devour. Resist him, firm in faith, knowing that the same experience of suffering is required of your brotherhood throughout the world"* (1 Pet. 5:8, 9).

"Now war arose in heaven, Michael and his angels fighting against the dragon; and the dragon and his angels fought, but they were defeated and there was no longer any place for them in heaven. And the great dragon was thrown down, that ancient serpent, who is called the Devil and Satan, the deceiver of the whole world—he was thrown down to earth, and his angels were thrown down with him" (Rev. 12:7-9).

1. What kind of disguises does the devil use?
2. Who wins every time God's forces fight against Satan?
3. Are you resisting Satan "in faith" or in your own strength?

Undercover Agent

God is always associated with light. The devil is associated with darkness. Boogy men, monsters, headless horsemen, and goblins flourish at night but never seem to make appearances in daylight. That's because in darkness nonexistent things can appear to be real. The fear that plagued you at midnight will usually vanish as sunlight streams through your window the next morning. Most crimes are committed by night because people would be afraid or ashamed to do such things in broad daylight.

The Bible tells us there will be no night in heaven. Jesus will be its light.

The devil wants to blind you to the truth and make you live in darkness. You need to know that the devil has been defeated by Jesus on the cross and his doom is certain. The devil has already lost the war but wants to win some battles. He works as an undercover agent. His greatest weapons are deception and surprise.

By late 1944 Hitler's defeat was certain, but he wanted one last victory. He had several German soldiers dress up in American uniforms. They directed the American army the wrong way after road

signs had been changed. They then staged a surprise attack which is now known as the Battle of the Bulge.

One American unit was entirely surrounded. However, the commander of that unit, Brigadier General Antony McAuliffe, knew the score. He knew that the United States would win the war even if the present circumstances seemed the worst possible. His reply to the German demand to surrender was, "Nuts." That reply made history.

Satan's deception is like Hitler's scheme. He wants you to believe that the Bible isn't trustworthy, that God will never forgive you again, that your problem is too big for God, or that you can't hold out because you're surrounded by non-Christian people. You must learn to answer, "Nuts. I know that God is in charge of this universe. He will rescue me and help me."

"And this is the judgment, that the light has come into the world, and men loved darkness rather than light, because their deeds were evil. For every one who does evil hates the light, and

does not come to the light, lest his deeds should be exposed. But he who does what is true comes to the light, that it may be clearly seen that his deeds have been wrought [formed] *in God"* (John 3:19-21).

"Again Jesus spoke to them, saying, 'I am the light of the world; he who follows me will not walk in darkness, but will have the light of life' " (John 8:12).

1. What makes people hate light? Is there an area in your life that won't stand the test of God's spotlight? Confess it and get it straight with God.
2. Psalm 119:105 tells us that God's "word is a lamp to my feet and a light to my path." How can you use God's Word to add light to your life and prevent deception?

You'll Be Safe Inside the Tower

The Christian life is not a pleasure cruise; it's a fight. However, people often misunderstand the *nature* of this fight. The conflict is not against God, but against the devil.

Your unwillingness to break up with your non-Christian boyfriend, to be satisfied with the job God gave you, or to stay home from the camping trip because your mother needs your help are not examples of fighting the fight of faith. These things would be no problem if you surrendered completely to God and did whatever He asked you to do. If you are continually starting little revolutions against God's authority in your life, you'll be a walking civil war and in no condition to fight against Satan.

You must give God complete control of your life. Pray as the Psalmist, saying, "Unite my heart to fear thy name" (Ps. 86:11).

After you surrender to God, you must always remember that the battle against Satan can be won only by faith. If a fort or tower is strong enough, the person inside is absolutely safe. Our strong tower of defense is Jesus. We entered into Jesus, into this strong tower, by faith when we first accepted Jesus. By faith we are in Christ. The enemy can make no progress against our fortress.

The devil's strategy is to lure us out of the fortress and fight him out in the open, in which case we'll surely lose. Our first and greatest responsibility is to believe God, not to struggle and become exhausted with our trying. The person who trusts Jesus completely can endure the most difficult experience in victory and joy whether it be the death of a loved one, a serious accident, or unfair treatment by others. When we stop trusting, however, a flat tire, a bad grade, or a rainy day can become an immense trial.

Just because you stayed in the fortress and survived one big trial doesn't mean that the devil can't lure you into the "Field of Little Faith" for the next encounter. Remember, faith is the victory that overcomes the world.*

"The Lord is my rock, and my fortress, and my deliverer, my God, my rock, in whom I take refuge, my shield, and the horn of my salvation, my stronghold. I call upon the Lord, who is worthy to be praised, and I am saved from my enemies" (Ps. 18:2, 3).

"Hear my cry, O God, listen to my prayer; from the end of the earth I call to thee, when my heart is faint. Lead thou me to the rock that is higher than I; for thou art my refuge, a strong tower against the enemy" (Ps. 61:1-3).

1. How does the devil try to lure *you* into the "Field of Little Faith"?
2. List all the things God can be for you. Are you letting God be your security or are you trying to establish your own security?

---

*From a hymn by John Yates.

Take the Offensive

The best defense is a good offense. Often we become so concerned about the "don't's" in the Christian life that we forget the "do's." These "do's" can be summed up in the words, "You shall be holy, for I am holy" (1 Pet. 1:16).

Holiness is a hate for sin, an enthusiasm for what is right. But only the Holy Spirit can make us holy. That is why He is called the *Holy* Spirit. Since the only one who is truly holy is the Lord, you'll have as much of holiness as you have of God in you.

You may be asking, "How can I become holy?"

You must have a genuine desire for a holy life, a longing to hate sin and a willingness to give up anything God asks you to give up. You'll also want God to give you enthusiasm and power to *enjoy* doing right.

You probably recognize that none of this will come from within you. It must be God's action—you simply cooperate. You must believe that God will accomplish His work in you, since He has commanded you to be holy.

In today's fast-moving, pleasure-seeking society, making holiness your top priority won't be easy or popular. But it is the way to victory.

> "Take time to be holy,
> The world rushes on;
> Spend much time in secret
> With Jesus alone;
> By looking to Jesus
> Like Him thou shalt be;
> Thy friends in thy conduct
> His likeness shall see."*

"For this very reason make every effort to supplement your faith with virtue, and virtue with knowledge, and knowledge with self-control, and self-control with steadfastness, and steadfastness with godliness, and godliness with brotherly affection, and brotherly affection with love. For if these things are yours and abound, they keep you from being ineffective or unfruitful in the knowledge of our Lord Jesus Christ. For whoever lacks these things is blind and shortsighted and has forgotten that he was cleansed from his old sins. Therefore, brethren, be the more zealous [enthusiastic] to confirm your call and election, for if you do this you will never fall" (2 Pet. 1:5-10).

1. How can you take the offensive so as to make Christian virtues part of your life?
2. How much enthusiasm do you have for living your life only to please Jesus?
3. Ask Jesus if there is something specific that He wants to change in your life.

---

*Words by William Longstaff.

You Must Supply the Mold

You probably agree that "overcoming evil with good" is logical and scriptural. However, you may still wonder how you can live a holy life without entering a monastery or camping on an uninhabited South Pacific island where there are no drug pushers, porno magazines, or temptations to quarrel with your sister. Well, there is a way. You can cooperate with God so that He can give you His holiness.

The holiness God wants to give you is like a foundation for your Christian life. The foundation of a traditional house is not made from wood. However, the enduring, strong cement must be poured into wooden forms. Now, you can't make yourself holy, but you can provide the forms for God's holiness. Your longing to be holy, your willingness to spend time with God, your turning away from sin, and your determination to follow Jesus regardless of the cost are the forms into which God will pour His holiness.

The molds for God's holiness are very practical things. Suppose your sister borrows your new sweater without asking and spills spaghetti sauce on it. Your determination to love and forgive her is a form for God's holiness.

Suppose that everyone else is easily learning to play racquetball and you can't even return one serve. You can then decide to keep calm and trust God so that He can give you His grace and His peace.

God will show you what He is like and how to be like Him as you spend time in prayer and Bible study each day. As you supply more molds, turning down the invitation to attend a wild party, fouling out of an important game graciously, praising God in spite of that D on the physics test, and obeying your father even if your friends laugh at you, God's holiness will fill your molds.

"Since we have these promises, beloved, let us cleanse ourselves from every defilement [everything filthy or dirty] *of body and spirit, and make holiness perfect in the fear of God"* (2 Cor. 7:1).

"Strive for peace with all men, and for the holiness without which no one will see the Lord" (Heb. 12:14).

"His divine power has granted to us all things that pertain to life and godliness, through the knowledge of him who called us to his own glory and excellence, by which he has granted to us his precious

and very great promises, that through these you may escape from the corruption that is in the world because of passion, and become partakers of the divine nature" (2 Pet. 1:3, 4).

1. What do these verses teach you about the molds which you are to construct for God's holiness?
2. According to Hebrews 12:14, what is the implied reward for holiness?
3. In 2 Peter 1:3, 4, what things has God promised to give to us?

Your Personal Body, Soul, and Spirit Guard

Jesus wants to be your personal body, soul, and spirit guard, but you must stay close enough to Him so He can guard you. The Psalm writer says, "Because he cleaves to me in love, I will deliver him; I will protect him, because he knows my name" (Ps. 91:14).

The devil is always trying to get you out from under God's protection. He distorts scripture so you won't wholeheartedly obey Jesus. Like Eve, we all find it easy to listen to such distortions and reason ourselves into a lot of trouble. For instance, the Bible says that "love is not resentful" and commands us to love everybody, even our enemies. Satan will help you rationalize that it's all right to dislike the girl who stole your boyfriend, the guy who constantly puts you down, and people who boss you around for no reason.

However, "love is not resentful" is God's truth. If you don't root resentment out of your life, the devil will see that weak spot and send in his "What to Think About Demons" named Hate, Get Even, and Self-pity. Unless you reject these, you'll soon be saying and doing things you didn't think you were capable of.

The devil's version of Ephesians 4:29 is, "Let no evil talk come out of your mouths—sometimes." Statements such as, "This isn't very nice, but it's the truth," "I shouldn't say this, but I know you won't tell anybody," and "I probably shouldn't repeat it, but," all come from the book called *Christian Living Made Easy* by Lucifer and Company. The devil's lie that your situation is an exception to God's Word opens the floodgates of criticism, false rumors, and gossip.

This can be avoided if you stay close to Jesus. Obey His every word, love Him better than anyone else and give Him complete control of your life. Jesus wants to guard you and keep you from evil. He will if you're not out doing your own thing.

"Love the Lord, all you his saints! The Lord preserves the faithful, but abundantly requites [repays] *him who acts haughtily* [with pride]*"* (Ps. 31:23).

"The Lord loves those who hate evil; he preserves the lives of his saints; he delivers them from the hand of the wicked" (Ps. 97:10).

"The Lord preserves all who love him; but all the wicked he will destroy" (Ps. 145:20).

1. What kind of attitudes do we need to have in order to claim God's promises of protection?
2. Are there any sins you're hanging onto by rationalizing your behavior? What steps should you take to obey God fully?

Week Thirteen

LIFE'S UPS AND DOWNS

To Jesus, with Love

What do you think when you hear phrases such as "total conse-cration," "full surrender," or "giving your life completely to Jesus"? Possibly you picture raising your hand at a meeting and go-ing forward or selling all your possessions and giving to the poor. Maybe the whole idea scares you.

One of the devil's chief lies is that God is a big meanie; that as soon as you surrender your life to Him, He will send you straight to Zambia, that He'll tell you to give up chocolate-chip cookies for-ever, and force you to learn Hebrew.

Suppose a little boy came running to his father and said, "Daddy, I love you so much I'll do anything you ask me to do." The father wouldn't reply, "That's just what I've been waiting for. I'm locking you in the closet for twenty-four hours. When you get out, you'll have to eat spinach three times a day, and will never be al-lowed to play baseball again." Even the worst earthly father wouldn't respond this way and certainly God wouldn't.

On the other hand, the father of the three-year-old wouldn't cancel all dental appointments because the boy hated the dentist. God *will* give us His best if we surrender our lives totally to Him. But everything will not necessarily seem best at the time and be ut-terly enjoyable.

Giving your life completely to Jesus may seem imposssible and impractical. That Jesus expects absolute commitment to himself is clear in Scripture. Maybe you feel that the demand is something you can't attain. Remember that you are not under the law which demands but gives no power to fulfill. You are under grace (God's special favor and strength enabling us to do things we could not ac-complish otherwise). The grace of God within gives you the power to surrender yourself totally to God. If you try to do it in your own strength, your knuckles will turn white from hanging on for dear life.

Give your life to Jesus because you love Him and you know He loves you.

"He who loves father or mother more than me is not worthy of me; and he who loves son or daughter more than me is not worthy of me; and he who does not take his cross and follow me is not worthy

of me. He who finds his life will lose it, and he who loses his life for my sake will find it" (Matt. 10:37-39).

"Another said, 'I will follow you, Lord; but let me first say farewell to those at my home.' Jesus said to him, 'No one who puts his hand to the plow and looks back is fit for the kingdom of God'" (Luke 9:61, 62).

1. Is there anyone or anything you love more than you love Jesus? Is there anything you want to do before you give Jesus your whole life?
2. What does Jesus think about us putting other people and things before Him?
3. What is the reward of "losing your life" for Jesus?

Are You Willing to Stay on the Altar?

As you commit yourself to Jesus, you'll discover the need for ever deeper levels of consecration. You commit to Him now everything that you are and have. However, you may not be the least aware of the fact that your sense of humor is offensive to Jesus; but when the Holy Spirit shows you this, you must give it over to Him. Later, He may point out that you manipulate people even though you never realized it before. Then you must give this over to Jesus and determine to stop it.

Each time you gain a new position or possession, you must ask the Holy Spirit how to give it completely to Jesus. Last year you didn't have to think about how to give being captain of the football team to Jesus. This year you will. You may suddenly find yourself needing to know how to give your boyfriend and your dating relationship to Jesus. God requires of us a "living sacrifice"—a daily giving of our lives to Jesus.

Someone has remarked that the trouble with a living sacrifice is that it keeps trying to crawl off the altar. Confess your sin immediately when you sense you're trying to take back the commitment you've made. Give it all to God. Your living sacrifice is made to your living Lord. Your close relationship and personal attachment to

Him are the secret of being a living sacrifice and loving it.

"I appeal to you therefore, brethren, by the mercies of God, to present your bodies as a living sacrifice, holy and acceptable to God, which is your spiritual worship" (Rom. 12:1).
"Brethren, do not be weary in well-doing" (2 Thess. 3:13).
"For Demas [one of Paul's co-workers], *in love with this present world, has deserted me and gone to Thessalonica"* (2 Tim. 4:10).
1. What does it mean to be a "living sacrifice"?
2. What things can prevent us from being a living sacrifice?
3. What choices that you make will determine if you become like Demas?

Mountaintops

You probably remember the day you became a Christian. You were so happy you thought you'd never have another problem. You may also recall a retreat or a Bible camp where you felt very close to God. Maybe at one point you surrendered yourself completely to God and experienced the supernatural power of the Holy Spirit. You saw clearly for the first time how much God loved you and realized that you could trust Him for everything.

Each valid Christian experience comes from a revelation [a revealing] of God's truth. We have to understand that Jesus died for our sins before we can personally accept Jesus. We have to see that God loves us completely before we can yield our lives totally to Him. We have to know that Jesus' Spirit within us can overcome sin before we think we can live a victorious life.

First we know something, then we act on it. Often this action is a crisis or "mountaintop" experience. But after scaling the peak we must face entering the valley. After surrendering your life to Christ, you must still go back to Mr. Green's art class, talk to your father about borrowing the car, and face your old boyfriend or girlfriend.

There is no Christian experience that will exempt you from walking close to Jesus day by day. There is no experience that will stay bright and glowing and allow you to ignore God and go your own way.

The temptation of thinking that now you can sit back and relax is a real one—one the devil uses on a lot of sincere Christians. The real test is living day by day in the new light, insight, and power you have received. The way to do this is always the same. Spend time praying and reading the Bible each day. Talk everything over with God. Build a deep relationship with Him. Determine that nothing, not even good things, will take up so much of your time, energy, brain power, or emotional involvement that God will ever take second place.

"As therefore you received Christ Jesus the Lord, so live in him" (Col. 2:6).

"Not that I have already obtained this or am already perfect; but I press on to make it my own, because Christ Jesus has made me his own. Brethren, I do not consider that I have made it my own; but one thing I do, forgetting what lies behind and straining forward to what lies ahead, I press on toward the goal for the prize of the upward call of God in Christ Jesus. Only let us hold true to what we have attained" (Phil. 3:12-14, 16).

1. Paul didn't believe that he was Mr. Perfect. Why shouldn't a Christian feel that he or she has "arrived"?
2. List the right attitudes that Christians should have.
3. Why should we hold onto what we've already attained (learned and experienced)?

Falling Off Cloud Nine and Other High Places

Are you a "superstar Christian" one day but blow it the next day? Just when you think you've made a spiritual giant step, do you fail miserably? Has the devil ever whispered to you, "You're such a lousy Christian you might as well give up"? Falling short of *your* goal is not failure in the Christian life. Failure is falling short of *God's* requirement.

The fact of failure is not nearly as important as your attitude toward it. There are two extremes to avoid. The first is *discourage-*

ment. No verse in the Bible says that because you failed, God doesn't love you or want you anymore. Don't ever believe that lie. Don't decide that you must not really be a Christian just because you messed up.

The other extreme is flippancy. The attitude, "Well, I bombed again. Big deal," is not God's will either. Saying, "I might as well learn to accept failure since I'll fail all the time anyway" is very dangerous. It's saying that God is so weak that He cannot keep you from failing.

Parents expect their child who is learning to walk to take a few tumbles. Even so, as you mature spiritually there will be growing pains and falls. But your Heavenly Father watches your progress with the same joy that earthly parents have when their child learns something new. God is always there with comfort for the child who needs it. The child who stumbles doesn't fail to learn to walk. That could only happen if the child refused to try again.

The reason you fail is because you have not relied on Jesus in complete faith. Jesus never fails and if He is directing your life, you will not stumble. His path for you might not lead to success that the world will admire, but it will please God.

"The steps of a man are from the Lord, and he establishes him in whose way he delights; though he fall, he shall not be cast headlong, for the Lord is the stay of his hand" (Ps. 37:23, 24).

"But the Lord is faithful; he will strengthen you and guard you from evil" (2 Thess. 3:3).

"Now to him who is able to keep you from falling and to present you without blemish before the presence of his glory with rejoicing, to the only God, our Savior through Jesus Christ our Lord, be glory, majesty, dominion, and authority, before all time and now and forever" (Jude 1:24, 25).

1. If we fail, what do you think is the reason?
2. What promise can we claim if we do fail?
3. List all the things God wants to do for us if we completely trust and obey Him. Which of these do you need most right now? Ask God to help you claim this promise by faith.

The Unnecessary F's on Your Christian Report Card

The Christian who says, "I always fail," should remember a couple of things. One is that you should expect failure from *yourself.* The devil is always stronger than you are when alone. The other thing is that if you totally rely on God for every situation, you will not fail.

Trusting God and relying on Him totally is a learning experience. We are so accustomed to doing a million things without even a thought of God. He must therefore show us our weakness—sometimes through many minor catastrophes. Sometimes we need many such reminders.

It is a fact that flour, sugar, shortening, baking powder, milk, eggs and vanilla in proper proportion will make a cake batter. It may be a Betty Crocker no-fail blue-ribbon recipe. However, if I don't believe I could make a nice, high, fluffy cake by following a recipe, I won't even try. But I could knowingly or unknowingly change the recipe and have a failure. When the pancake-like layers are taken from the oven, I shouldn't throw the cookbook out the window. I should re-check the recipe to see what I did wrong.

Take all your failures to Jesus. Confess your lack of faith to Him. Ask for wisdom if you don't really know what went wrong. He'll gently teach you how to trust Him. God will keep you from falling if you cooperate by being watchful, diligent, and full of faith. You must always keep your mind on Jesus.

"May the God of peace himself sanctify you wholly; and may your spirit and soul and body be kept sound and blameless at the coming of our Lord Jesus Christ. He who calls you is faithful, and he will do it" (1 Thess. 5:23, 24).

"For we do not want you to be ignorant, brethren, of the affliction we experienced in Asia; for we were so utterly, unbearably crushed that we despaired of life itself. Why, we felt that we had received the sentence of death; but that was to make us rely not on ourselves but on God who raises the dead; he delivered us from so deadly a peril, and he will deliver us; on him we have set our hope that he will deliver us again" (2 Cor. 1:8-11).

"For he has said, 'I will never fail you nor forsake you' " (Heb. 13:5).

1. List the promises of God stated in these verses.
2. What should every crushing problem and failure make us do?
3. The Jesus who does not fail lives inside you. It's your job to make sure that the life of Jesus within you finds expression in the way you live your life. What things in your personality prevent your friends from seeing Jesus in you? In what ways can you help Jesus express himself through you?

How to Run the Rat Race Without Becoming a Rat

Do you ever feel like screaming, "Stop the world. I want to get off"? Does the fast pace, the time squeeze, and the list of things to be done drive you up a wall?

The answer to this dilemma, as well as all others, can be found in the guidance and power of the Holy Spirit. As always, Jesus is our supreme example. He spent unhurried time in prayer and received the guidance of the Holy Spirit. He could therefore handle the crowds and the many demands placed upon Him. He knew when to "get away from it all" in order to spend time alone with God in prayer.

There were many unhealed lepers, many who had not heard Jesus preach, and many who had rejected Him. Yet He could say to God, "I glorified thee on earth, having accomplished the work which thou gavest me to do" (John 17:4). He received His orders from God and didn't jump from one thing to another deciding on His own what to do. He did only what God told Him to do.

Put faith in the fact that the Holy Spirit does live in you and He will direct you. The person receiving directions must be quiet, must concentrate, and listen attentively. This is where so many of us in this activity-oriented society fall down. We have difficulty being quiet long enough for the Holy Spirit to speak to us.

Unfortunately, most prayer is a one-way conversation. We dictate to God our shopping list and say "Amen." If we really want the peace of God, we can't come to our devotions with the attitude of a rat making a quick pit stop before rejoining the race. The Bible

talks about "waiting on God," and waiting is something most of us are not very good at. But unless we wait before God until we can clearly hear His instructions, we'll never experience His direction in our lives.

Whether you choose to run the rat race like any other rat is up to you, but there is a way out.

"And in the morning, a great while before day, [Jesus] rose and went out to a lonely place, and there he prayed" (Mark 1:35).

"And great multitudes gathered to hear and to be healed of their infirmities. But he withdrew to the wilderness and prayed" (Luke 5:15, 16).

"For thus said the Lord God, the Holy One of Israel, 'In returning and rest you shall be saved; in quietness and in trust shall be your strength' " (Isa. 30:15).

"And the effect of righteousness will be peace, and the result of righteousness, quietness and trust forever" (Isa. 32:17).

1. What do you do when things are piling up and the pressure is on? What *should* you do?
2. Right living results in peace. In order to live right you must spend time with God and find out what He wants you to do. Are you willing to make that time with God a priority?

If the Volume Is Up Too High, You Can't Hear the Still Small Voice

If you and your boyfriend or girlfriend wish to clear up a misunderstanding, you don't arrange for a quick interview during a time out of the Super Bowl game! A marriage proposal is not generally made at a bustling railroad station when the young man must catch his train in five minutes.

We recognize that important discussions with other people need time and peaceful surroundings. Yet many of us approach our communication with God on a "five minutes with God and I won't turn off the TV. I might miss something" basis. Often we don't stay before God in prayer long enough for our minds to forget about the lost billfold or the last family quarrel.

Have you ever spent a half hour in absolute quietness before Jesus? Try it. It's wonderful. That unhurried quiet time is necessary if the Holy Spirit is to direct your everyday life. The more busy you are, the more you need this quiet time before God.

Martin Luther reportedly remarked, "I have so much business I cannot get on without spending three hours daily in prayer."

Andrew Murray advises, "Sit down every morning, sit down often in the day and say, 'Lord Jesus, I know nothing. I will be silent. Let the Spirit lead me.'"

To hear the voice of God you must be deaf to other voices—the voices of your friends, the media, and your own desires. If you're so busy that there isn't quiet, unhurried time for prayer, the Holy Spirit can't speak to you.

If you're going to get up early to have a quiet time with God, you'll have to go to bed earlier at night. Something you enjoy doing, something that is not wrong, may have to be cut out.

Deciding to make quiet time with God a priority will be extremely difficult. Even other Christians won't understand. People will think it weird that a normal red-blooded teenager would give up something fun or profitable to spend time with God.

God has some very important things to say to you. You'll never hear them unless you turn down the volume and stop long enough to listen.

"And behold, the Lord passed by, and a great and strong wind

*rent the mountains, and broke in pieces the rocks before the Lord,
but the Lord was not in the wind; and after the wind an earthquake,
but the Lord was not in the earthquake; and after the earthquake a
fire, but the Lord was not in the fire: and after the fire a still small
voice. And the Lord said to* [Elijah], *'Go. . .'* " (1 Kings 19:11b, 12,
15a).

*"But they who wait for the Lord shall renew their strength, they
shall mount up with wings like eagles, they shall run and not be
weary, they shall walk and not faint"* (Isa. 40:31).

1. Why would the mountain be a good place for God to talk to Elijah? Ask God to help you find your "mountain," that quiet place where you can talk to Him. It might take a miracle, but God is very good at performing miracles!
2. The wind and the earthquake and the fire represent our strong emotions and reactions to life's circumstances. Why can't God speak to us through these?
3. Are you willing to stay before God long enough to hear His still small voice and to have your strength renewed?